Twice as Different

Twice as Different

a novel

KL PALMER

WordCrafts Press

Twice as Different
Copyright © 2015
KL Palmer

Cover concept and design by Mike Parker

ISBN: 978-1-962218-05-4

Published by WordCrafts Press
Cody, Wyoming 82414
www.wordcrafts.net

To mamas everywhere

Whether you are single, married, divorced or widowed.
From moms-to-be, to mothers of kids who have had kids who had
kids.
It takes a village.
We may be perfect and at times we may feel like giving up.
But we are united.
Moms, mommies, mothers, stepmoms, adoptive moms, foster moms,
and those who helped raised children like moms they needed.
You are loved. You are appreciated. You are amazing humans.
Never forget that.

I wasn't exactly young when I became a mother. I was however, single for the most part. I had just turned twenty-two when my baby girls were born. I was alone in the hospital when the contractions grew to stiff mountain peaks on the monitor. I didn't realize how alone I was though, because a team of nurses and doctors hurried to prepare for their arrival.

I didn't miss having a partner's hand to hold. I only worried about pain and when my parents would arrive. In the end, they were fourteen minutes late for the main event.

As a history major in college I didn't hesitate when naming them. My old-fashioned heart was torn between two famous *and attractive* men from history. Neither one of them was alive anymore, so I couldn't claim either as the mysterious father of his love child.

Presley beat her sister Kennedy by two minutes. I guess by the timeline of their lives, Elvis was actually born later, but the way she curled her lip before she cried made my decision before I could even think about my choice.

Kennedy was named for the best president I've known *or would ever know as far as I'm concerned.* No, I didn't ever get to witness him personally give speeches and only really learned about him when given his presidency to research for a high school history class report; but he was so amazingly good looking I didn't really care what he had to say.

Yes, I, Pamela Jean Taylor was twenty-two years old, alone and raising two baby girls. Their father was Tim something. I don't remember what his name was, only that his tracks left fire as he ran from town the minute he found out I was pregnant. I heard he had joined the Air Force. My girls would spend the next 16 ½ years thinking he never made it back from war. There might be truth in that. I didn't know. And I had no way of finding out. I hadn't planned on getting pregnant. But isn't that what all people involved in unplanned pregnancies say? As I looked at their faces, so perfect, so precious, none of that mattered. I wouldn't give them up. Nurses had to pry them from my arms to bathe them, change them, or to quickly take their measurements.

"Bet you'll do more with them than that silly History degree," my dad said when finally arriving at the hospital.

He was right. Three quarters of the way through school I had no idea what I would do with that degree and didn't even want to finish. I only did because I had a full ride scholarship from being valedictorian of my high school. I giggled to myself wondering what the class would think of their leader now… practically poor with not one but two babies. I didn't care. I was so thrilled. I loved my girls. As I watched them sleep I cried with delight.

My parents were wonderful about the whole experience. Where they should have preached or could have lectured they calmly guided me along the path of motherhood. They were older when they had me but were secretly excited to get to know their grandchildren before they were too old to enjoy them. And it remained a secret until the day I heard mom rocking them late at night telling them that exact thing.

For the next four years we lived with my parents, the electrifying Janice and somber Ed Taylor. I was a front desk clerk for a local car dealership, and my mom helped with the girls during the day while I was at work.

The same month that they turned four I received a call that I've been waiting for. Even though I didn't get an offer for a job using my college education, I did get the interview I'd been hoping for. The position was the executive assistant role to the CFO of a major corporate office. The bad news was that if I was offered the position I would need to move to the other side of the state. I loved Virginia, but there were a lot of miles from the western side where I was raised to the eastern coast line, where the position was.

All too quickly a decision would need to be made. I was told that the job was mine if I wanted it. Money talked, and the dollar signs flashing in front of my eyes made my mind up for me. My girls and I packed up and were moved within three weeks. The following Monday after arriving in Wellington Beach near the Virginia/North Carolina coastline. I walked into the 34th floor lobby of my new life.

Twelve years later I still smile as I did that day. I love my job and enjoy coming into work every day.

So why am I now leaving the building in utter fury? Well, that reason is named Presley. Ten minutes before this moment, I received a call from Deputy Warren at the county Sherriff's office. After confirming I was her mother I listened to the husky male voice on the other end tell me how my daughter ended up in his office. She and an eighteen-year-old unnamed male were brought in for underage drinking. It was 11:20 in the morning! She was supposed to be at school! And just who was this eighteen-year-old male?

Chapter Two

Presley was sitting with her arms crossed and slouched in a plastic chair in the middle of a crowded holding area. Her face, streaked with tears, was wretched in anger. A boy sat beside her with a dragon tattooed down the length of his forearm. He was chewing the side of his thumb and staring off into space looking more scared than she did.

"Mommy!" She jumped up from her seat knocking it backwards.

"Do not *Mommy* me!" I said through clenched teeth. After squinting and sighing deeply in the direction of the boy, I continued, "And we will talk about *him* later."

Presley apologized the four long miles home. She promised to clean the house, ground herself, and never, ever, ever to do it again…. As long as I didn't hurt or make her stop seeing Rob.

Ah! Rob! That's the name of Dragon Boy.

"No can do pumpkin. You will *never* see him again. Never, ever, ever," I mocked her.

Seconds later I heard her bedroom door slam.

Minutes after that, her door was taken off the hinges, and she was forced to look at my disappointed face.

She growled and threw herself face down on her bed. I simply walked away twirling the screwdriver between my fingers listening to muffled screams that fell silent in her furry purple pillow.

Being a mom was hard. Choosing to do it alone was an even bigger feat. But being a mom of a rebelling teenage girl was virtually impossible to master.

I sank deep into the couch and laid my head on the cushioned back. Just as I closed my eyes the front door banged open.

My eyes flew open, and I slowly turned toward the door. There was Kennedy biting her bottom lip to keep from crying. She took in a slow breath, and I watched her lips quiver.

"Are you okay?" I asked her, sitting up.

"It's Becca's cat ... it was ... it's ... the poor thing was hit by a car mom. What's worse? We had to see that from the bus window," she explained, and before she could stop it the dam of tears broke loose.

All I could do was sit there, shake my head, and think, *How can two girls—twin girls—be so incredibly and completely different.*

I listened to her sob as she climbed the stairs. Her footsteps disappeared into her room on the left, and just like her sister she threw herself on her bed.

Lexi and Luke, our two Jack Russell terriers raced into the room from the kitchen. Both jumped up on their hind legs and danced around at my feet. They knew I needed a laugh to calm down. I applauded them, and they thanked me in return by wagging their little tails.

Lexi rolled over, and I scratched her furry belly. Satisfied with my brief attention both pups jumped to the couch and lay on my lap. I stroked them blindly while once again closing my eyes.

The excitement in the air disappeared, and the house was now extremely quiet. Just as I was drifting off for a nap, a knock at the front door jolted me awake. Both dogs jumped simultaneously to the floor and barked furiously warning me of the unknown visitor.

Now what? I thought.

As I opened the door I noticed the bowed pitiful head of Rob, the Dragon boy delinquent.

"I'm sorry Mrs. Taylor. Everything is my fault. Okay? I just really want to still be able to see Pres—"

He was cut off by the sound of the front door shutting.

"That's *Ms.* Taylor Dragon boy," I said to the wooden door.

"Mom who was that?" Presley had emerged from her door-less room and was standing at the top of the stairs.

"Oh nobody. Just someone trying to sell something. Don't worry. I quickly told him I'm not buying it."

Chapter Three

Going back to work the next day was a much needed relief for me. Earlier that morning, Kennedy sat quietly at the breakfast table, upset, and still sporting red-rimmed eyes from crying about the cat. Yes, it was considered a *neighborhood pet* in that everyone fed it, but I honestly considered it more of a nuisance after catching it numerous times on my car from the telltale paw prints left behind. I also knew that Becca, who has been Kennedy's best friend since kindergarten, was devastated. She had just lost her childhood pet.

I kissed the top of her head as I passed her walking to the coffee maker. She sighed dramatically.

"I promise your day will only get better," I encouraged her.

She simply sighed again in response.

Presley, on the other hand, was still not speaking to me. I was perfectly fine with that since I knew if I did say anything to her it would be said with a *what were you thinking?* or *I'm so disappointed in you* included in the comment. It was best to just wait.

"Do you have dance practice this afternoon?" I asked her while pouring coffee in a to-go cup.

She grunted.

"That a yes?"

She grunted again.

"Okay then, well grunt again if you need me to pick you up from practice." I added creamer and stirred slowly waiting for her answer.

She rolled her eyes, and as she stood to walk away I answered for her. "Okay, even though no response must mean you don't want me to, I'll still be there at 5:30 to pick you up."

I kissed her on the head before she could fully stand up.

She grunted in reply.

I followed them out the door and yelled my good-byes, getting a smile and wave from Kennedy and sneer from Presley. I knew she would be better by the end of the day. The girls rarely held grudges for too long.

Taking a long drag from my steaming mug, I sank down into the front seat of my car and prepared for the long day ahead of work. There has been a lot of tension building in the office, and my boss had scheduled back-to-back meetings all day. I knew the small amount of peace I had in the commute into town would be the most I would probably have all day.

Chapter Four

I had exactly 3.45 seconds to turn my laptop and desk lamp on before the first meeting's guests arrived. They were 12 minutes early. My boss, Mr. Stevenson, hadn't even arrived yet; but it didn't seem to bother them. One gentleman talked quietly on his cellphone while the other looked through his briefcase, pulling files out and sorting papers frantically.

Leaving them to wait, I prepared the conference room, restocking the snacks and cold drinks and making a fresh pot of coffee. I opened the blinds and filled pitchers with ice water. I was just finishing up when I heard Mr. Stevenson walk in the front followed quickly by two operation managers who worked in the same office. They hurriedly said their greetings, shook hands, and I arrived by their side just in time to escort them into the conference room.

While the group spent the next couple hours with the first two visitors, I made reservations for a lunch meeting they had across town and prepared a financial presentation for the afternoon meeting that was scheduled.

As I worked through the pages, there were noticeably a lot of red-bolded negative numbers. I didn't give much thought to what they meant or what the meeting was even about. I simply wanted to get finished with what Mr. Stevenson needed so I could tackle the inbox that was now overflowing on my desk.

I suppose if I had paid more attention to that financial presentation and all those bright, glaring red numbers I wouldn't have been so shocked when I got the call to go into Mr. Stevenson's office at 3:45 that afternoon.

I think my jaw not only hit the floor but bounced off of it with the news he had to tell me 3.45 minutes later. My position was eliminated due to an unforeseen and immediate downsizing.

As I ran through the day's events in my mind I found a maniacal laugh escape from my lips. 3.4.5—not my luckiest numbers that day.

Chapter Five

I drove home in a daze. I turned the radio off and listened to myself breathe, and thoughts slam around inside my busy head. I blinked, only vaguely aware of the road and traffic around me. It's good to know that when your mind is so flooded with stress there is a Higher Power that gets you home in one piece.

I sat in the car for ten minutes after parking in the driveway, still blinking to the beat of my heart. It was just after 4:30. I had left as soon as I walked out of Mr. Stevenson's office. I hadn't even stopped to turn off the computer. I knew tears would fall, and I wanted to be in my car when it happened. I had an hour to spare before picking up Presley from dance, so I wanted to just be alone to cry and make sure my eyes were dry and no longer puffy before I had to go to the school.

But tears surprisingly didn't come. I guess my body at that moment was too stunned to allow it. Instead I sat in the driveway and just closed my eyes. I let out a painful sigh, and when I opened my eyes back up, I was staring at a smiling, waving Kennedy. I forced a smile and got out of the car. She ran to hug me.

"You're home early. I'm so glad. I wanted to show you something." She dragged me into the house.

Leaving me to take off my shoes and put down my purse, she ran off to get me the surprise. I was just walking into the living room when she met me with a bright yellow folder. "I wanted to show you before Presley did." She shoved the packet in front of my face.

Focusing on the words on the top page of the stapled packet I realized it was the information for their junior trip to New York.

$1,200 a kid!

"Ugh…" I simply said dropping the folder onto the couch.

"It's a discount right now. If we wait just even a couple more months the price goes up to \$1,400. Because of that I think we should go ahead and sign up now," Kennedy reasoned the savings.

I sank down beside the folder and picked it back up trying to concentrate on what exactly it said. What bad timing this was.

"I understand what you're saying, but fund raising hasn't even started yet. I can't afford to just dish out \$2,400 for you girls—especially not now." I added in a whisper.

"But we *are* going, right?" she asked. "I mean you said…"

I cut her off. "Of course. I promised you after missing your freshman and sophomore trips that you would definitely go to your last two."

"Okay. Well don't forget about it, or we'll be paying extra." She skipped up the stairs leaving me with the folder to stare at.

I heard the splash of the tear hit the paper before I saw it. There it was. The tears. I knew they'd eventually come.

Chapter Six

I sat alone at the kitchen table listening to the soft ticking rhythm of the clock. I slowly stirred the spoon around in my hot tea. It was one o'clock in the morning, and the girls had been in their beds for hours.

I had entertained them with cooking, homework, sitting between them on the couch watching back-to-back movies, and finally helping to paint toe nails. It wasn't until they went upstairs that I realized I needed to take time to think, to shut off my mom brain.

With no television on and no distractions, I prepared for the bumper car affect the building questions took on in my brain. *Where would I go now? How do I start over? What was I truly going to do now?*

Most families would fall back on another income, or downsize, or the other spouse take a second job or more hours. I didn't have those options. Downsizing to us meant moving into a one bedroom apartment with a kitchenette on *the other side of the tracks.*

Mr. Stevenson described his offer of a severance package. I had to admit it was above and beyond what most people would probably get. I had been with him for so long that he promised to take care of me. I would keep my normal benefits and half my income for six months and then have the option to continue benefits at a higher premium after that. All I could think about was that small window of six months and the amount of money I'd need to compensate for the other half that was lost.

I had to tell the girls.

Kennedy would feel sorry for me and probably offer to quit lacrosse and find a job to help support the family. Presley would get mad, upset, and realize what she won't be able to buy now that the steady flow of funds to her pocket would end. She would probably ignore me for a few days and slowly come to terms with it, and we'd all fight through the tough times together.

I then instantly realized how tired I was. All these thoughts and plans were exhausting. I walked the ten feet to the couch and threw myself onto the throw pillows with a thud. I didn't even feel like crawling into bed that night.

Chapter Seven

My eyes slammed open in their sockets instantly giving me a headache. I blinked furiously to focus, realized my arm that was pinned under me was asleep, and sat up wondering what awoke me. After listening for a few seconds I realized there was fighting going on upstairs.

I shook the pins and needles from my arm and slowly carried my aching body up the stairs. *Why did I think sleeping on the couch was a good idea?* I asked myself as I ascended the stairs.

Presley was sitting in her bed, eyes rolled to the ceiling, sighing a response through her teeth to an unknown question. "But I *didn't* wear that dress!"

"Yes you did, stop lying," Kennedy pressed on shoving the garment into her face. "And you tore the belt off of it!"

"*I'm not lying, i didn't do it!*" Presley was now fully yelling in her sister's face.

I grabbed the dress, looked at the belt, and pursed my lips before speaking. "Presley, you *did* wear this dress two weeks ago, and you will fix it or buy her a new one. End of story." I threw the dress into her lap.

"I won't…I," Presley started to answer but I interrupted.

"*No, you will. I said end of story!*" I yelled, and both kids looked at me with wide eyes.

I never yelled. I'm not the mom that has to. One kid minds me no matter what, and one tries me until her power runs out and then I'm ignored. In both situations I'm civil.

I turned and quickly left the room, embarrassed by my loudness.

Kennedy quietly followed and turned into her room.

I shook my head as I walked back downstairs.

I needed coffee.

Chapter Eight

It was Saturday, which meant pancakes or French toast. It was a tradition us Taylor girls had since the girls could eat solid foods. I left the decision up to them each week, and if they couldn't agree, which was the majority of the time, I decided. Today, instead of a steaming plate of flapjacks or a griddle of French toast, I had three kinds of cereal boxes and bowls set on the bar. I was sipping my coffee loudly and staring down at the smiling monkey on one of the boxes when Presley slid into the stool to my left. "Mom? What's wrong?"

Still holding the mug to my lips I turned toward her wondering where this child came from and where the usual Presley was hiding.

"Seriously?! You were crazy up there," she continued.

Ahh, there she is.

Kennedy joined us at the bar, leaning on her elbows across from me. The way they looked from the cereal boxes to me with concern made me feel like I was part of an intervention.

I chuckled inside before setting my mug down slowly.

"Okay girls, you want to know what's wrong? I guess there is no need to wait to tell you." I quickly gathered my thoughts before continuing. The girls leaned even closer to me.

"I lost my job. They are consolidating the business which means downsizing our office." I looked down at my still and creamy coffee, impressed with not a ripple moving on the surface. My nerves felt splintered, but the coffee proved otherwise.

Then I immediately let go of the handle as if the liquid would jump out at any second. In doing so, the glasslike surface quickly fractured, and I was back in the kitchen.

Presley spoke first. "Um, that's not good. I mean, what are you gonna do now?"

"I don't know. This is a new place for me. I've never been without a job. I just…don't know,"

Kennedy spoke, but only in a whisper. "Forget about the trip we talked about yesterday."

"Wait! That's not fair. We *need* to go," Presley interjected, standing quickly.

"No, we don't Pres. *You* need to think about other things that money could be used for. *You're* not being fair," Kennedy responded.

It was my turn to speak. "I know I promised, and I know it's not fair. That's why, come hell or high water you're going. That much is a sure thing."

Presley sat back down and crossed her arms, and we all just stared at one another in silence.

For the next few minutes nobody said anything. Neither girl commented on my remark about the trip. They each took a cereal box and silently filled bowls, no longer wondering where the pancakes or French toast were.

I broke the silence. "I'm looking for something first thing Monday morning. I'm sure there will be a job just waiting for me. I have a ton of office experience and nothing to lose."

I twirled my cup around and nodded, convinced I could get over the hurdle. I was right. I had nothing to lose. This should be easy.

Chapter Nine

Well that didn't happen like I thought it would. A job just waiting for me? Boy was I wrong! Three long weeks later there were still no calls with job offers. My confidence was all but gone. It had been dwindling for a while, and I felt now like I was quickly growing desperate.

While talking to my friend Bonnie, who worked for a small realtor in the area, she mentioned that they had a part-time job waiting in her office if I wanted it. The work involved processing deals, assisting in writing listings, and most importantly answering phones. I turned it down two weeks ago not wanting to settle for just part-time. But now I was desperate and on my way to her office planning how I would beg to take the job now.

The pay would clear my house payment but nothing else. I would need to find more work. For now, I just needed to get this job.

Bonnie was making copies at the back of the office when I walked up to the empty receptionist desk. "Someone needs to hire some help around here." I gave her a cock-eyed smile.

She chuckled while shuffling papers. "Well, it seems good help is hard to find, and when I do, they turn me down. Give me two seconds while I send these documents off for a client." She turned on her sharp stiletto heel and hurried back to her desk.

While waiting, I flopped into a low leather chair and watched the second hand of the clock on the wall tick time forward. I could hear muffled conversation on the other side of the door that led into the main office. A telephone rang, and there was repetitive clicking of a keyboard.

As I was gathering all the sounds around me, Bonnie burst through the door causing me to stand up.

She didn't even notice the startled look on my face, simply reached out to give me a much needed hug. I held a little longer than normal, and she knew something was wrong.

"Don't worry, the job is still yours if you want it," she whispered.

I just nodded and fought back the tears. She squeezed me tight again before finally releasing me. "So, Congratulations are in order then, and with that I think your new job requires a girls' night out at Hastings—and no objections because this girl is buying," she offered.

Who was I to turn down a friend? Plus, it wasn't often I got a new job.

Not often enough anyway.

Chapter Ten

"Do you really think you should be running off to celebrate at a bar when we don't have money?" Presley was as poignant as a snake to its prey.

I answered as calmly as I could, "I think that it's something I shouldn't have to explain to my children, but because I am in no mood to fight I can tell you that Bonnie wants to take me out to celebrate *and* pay for my dinner, not at a bar, even though the place we are going to might have one in it, but at a restaurant.

"You said you're going to Hastings—that's a bar."

Kennedy spoke up before I could, "Pres, if it was just a bar we couldn't get in. We had the lacrosse dinner there last year, remember?"

I didn't have to say anything else, just adjusted my sleeves on my blouse and made sure the tail of it was still tucked into my black pencil skirt. Then I slid my feet into my heels and grabbed my purse.

"You look good mom," Kennedy commented.

Defeated, Presley agreed.

"Thanks guys. Pizza's in the oven. It shouldn't be but a few more minutes. I'll be back in a little while."

I shut the door and leaned my back up against the cool surface. After taking a deep breath I walked the sidewalk to my car. I needed a drink after fighting yet another battle with that dramatic duo.

Chapter Eleven

I ordered lemonade instead. As I waited for Bonnie to return from the restroom, I thought of the girls. Kennedy got her sincere, quiet demeanor from me. I flocked towards friends similar to my own personality. Both my girls were friends with many people, not settling on a best friend. I was only ever close to one at a time. But Kennedy… she was the one to hold her friends closest to her heart.

On my first day of elementary school I didn't speak a word until Celia Ford, Cecelia to be exact, brushed arms with me, and I said I was sorry. She apologized in a quiet voice to me at the same time that I did to her, and we remained friends throughout the rest of our school days together, only growing apart the end of our junior year when she became the apple of the eye for the quarterback at the rival high school.

We were still friends, just not as close. The day they broke up and she came crying to my house I drove across the town to his football field and spray painted his name with a few obscenities from 40-yard line to 40-yard line. I fought for those I loved and what I believed in. In this way I see myself in Presley.

When I moved to Wellington Beach and met Bonnie, someone so similar to me we could be sisters, I never looked for friendship anywhere else. Who needed that drama? She was there for me. I was there for her.

From across the room she motioned to a waiter and mouthed 'he's hot' for me to see. I shook my head and chuckled. She sank into her seat and unfolded her napkin onto her lap as if nothing happened.

Throughout dinner we continued to talk and laugh, and it was hard to imagine that any stresses in this world could ever separate us or cause me to find another friend.

Chapter Twelve

With my left arm propped on the table I held my chin and slowly rubbed the pad of my thumb along my lips. I tapped the checkbook with my pen and stared through the documents in front of me. I tried to see my nervous legs bouncing under the table, pretending they were far away, even attached to someone else's body.

Only the sound of the whistling from the tea kettle brought me back to my kitchen. I dropped the pen and watched it roll over the edge of the table and bounce onto the floor, frustrated that even that couldn't go right.

It had been two and a half months since I started at the real estate office. I enjoyed the job, loved the people, and the office was only a few blocks away so I was always home early. The pay was another story. Bonnie helped me get more than an average person and having a good reference also got me the weekends off. But it, combined with my partial severance pay, still didn't quite cover all the bills that came in every month.

Christmas came and finally went, and we survived it. I'm not sure how. I guess because the girls knew this year would be tighter than others past. Now, as I was sitting here this January day, twenty-four hours from the cutoff of "early bird" pricing on the junior class trip I dreaded this day coming more than any holiday.

After writing this check the savings I had was now all but depleted. Enough would be left for the girls' birthday that March and *a…just one…* emergency. Nothing more.

And now that the holidays were over I would begin looking for another full time job, but like the dollars in my account, time was rapidly running out.

Chapter Thirteen

"Okay, we know about your job situation, but why is there no Mr. Man in your life?" Bonnie asked from across the table. We were at lunch in a diner not far from the office. It had been the first time we've gotten to go out since the night we had celebrated my new job months ago.

She had been showing houses to a client that day and asked me to join her between showings. I hated to leave the phone unattended, but she assured me that it would be okay. Everyone had to eat sometime.

"You know I've tried going down that road. Once bitten twice shy, yes… but three times was not the lucky charm for me." I answered before putting a large forkful of salad into my mouth.

She shook her head. "Actually I think the statute of limitation on that mess has passed. It's time for you to dust yourself off and try again."

She was referring to John Howard, a local bank manager. We dated for two years. He was a prince by the way he could sweep a girl off her feet in one quick swoop, but also a cheat and liar who eventually ran himself out of town with his indiscretions. That was a little over three years ago. In his wake he left unpaid debt with me and two confused girls at my home.

"No thank you. I need to find a way to support me and the girls before thinking about finding a guy." I laughed.

"You know, there's nothing wrong with letting someone support you guys."

"Umm, yeah there is. This girl won't ever look for a guy like that. I've been independent since birth. It's kinda my thing."

"You sure you aren't late for the Men Hater's Club meeting?" she whispered under her breath.

I finished wiping my mouth and pushed the empty plate to the edge of the table. "Nope. As president I set the meeting times. Don't worry. I won't recruit you for membership, but not all of us met our soul mates in elementary school."

We sat in silence a few minutes before Bonnie broke it by throwing her napkin at me. "It wasn't elementary school it was junior high."

I cocked my head dramatically to the side and gave her a *same difference* look. She answered with a laugh before I threw the napkin back and hit her directly in her open mouth.

Chapter Fourteen

Again. Silence. That is all I heard. I sat at the bar in the kitchen and listened, surprised by the lack of sound. I had just told Kennedy and Presley my intent to sell the house. There were questions of why, tears of sadness knowing their childhood home would be gone, and words of anger and resentment. I explained that this house was way more than we need—than we *ever* needed. There were four bedrooms and only three of us, an eat-in kitchen, a formal dining room, and a living room as well as a family room. That is just too many rooms; space paid for but never used.

I always wanted a smaller house, less to clean and an ability to be closer as a family. Plus, with the girls leaving after the following year for college it would be like living in a lonely, empty castle. It also didn't hurt that I worked at a realtor's office and found the best deal for a cute three bedroom, two bathroom Cape Cod a little further out of town. At 1,800 square feet it was just about half the size of the house we were in now. The house payment and insurance would be about half as much as well. There was really no need to think about it. I was in survival mode and trying to think of everything we could do to get by.

I strained again, listening. If the house was smaller I would be able to hear the noises I knew were happening. Presley was probably drowning out life with music while paging through a magazine. I would assume Kennedy, although unhappy, was downsizing her room using the move as an excuse to clean out her closet or donate unwanted items to charity. Boy, were they as different as night and day.

I looked down at Lexi and Luke who sat perked at attention at my feet. "At least you guys don't care, right?" I asked.

They danced around in response and then chased each other out of the room.

I grabbed the boxes for packing that I had been given from the local grocer. I labeled one 'Donate' and one 'Yard Sale.' Before I could think about listing this house on the market I had a lot to purge, not only for showing purposes but also for downsizing into a smaller space.

As I turned to open the first set of cabinet doors, two white streaks flew by sliding around the corner and knocking the boxes onto their sides.

"Okay, so you guys will miss running around in a big house. Guess I truly am on my own for this decision," I said aloud.

Chapter Fifteen

It was the morning of the girls' seventeenth birthday. They had requested the moon, but both knew they'd just be lucky to get one drawn on paper. I had other plans for them. With the money I saved and a pity gift from their visiting grandparents we were able to get them a very used car to share. I sat back on the porch beside my dad. He was the quiet, calm type, but today he was in an anxious mood. He couldn't wait until they got home to see their surprise. In his nervousness he would get out of the chair and pace awhile, each time walking to the car and buffing a spot here and picking a leaf off there. It didn't matter what he did though. The paint was still faded. The wheels were still dull, and the windows required a jiggle when rolling them down; by hand. But it was a car; a great gift. Something my parents never did for me. Nonetheless, I was very excited for them to get home from shopping with their grandma too.

"It could be hours dad. You know how she is in the mall," I said, rocking back and forth in my chair, watching him use his shirt as a polishing rag.

He looked at his watch and then came back to join me on the porch.

"I am glad you guys made it for their birthday," I told him.

"You know we'd visit more often if we could—and well you need us for all this," he answered, motioning to the car.

That wasn't the "you're welcome" I was expecting, but I ignored his comment and tried to continue a conversation. "I was thinking once the house sells I'd like to bring the girls over for a long weekend. They haven't been there since they were little—probably don't even remember the place."

He tightly pursed his lips together into a frown and squinted before nodding his head in confirmation. I knew that look as his *we'll see about that, yes I'm being sarcastic* look.

I knew I was probably grasping at straws. It had been two months since we put the 'For Sale' sign in the yard and not one call had come in about it yet. Bonnie said it was priced well, just nobody in the market. I knew that was the truth by the way the phone's ringing slowed down in the office, and my hours began to be cut. I couldn't let dad know I was almost on the verge of desperation. And with that thought came warm tears welling in my eyes.

"Pammy? Are you okay?" Dad asked.

I didn't know he was looking and was embarrassed for being caught. I quickly blinked, and the tears shot down my face. I wiped my cheeks with both my hands like a child. "I'm just thinking about how they will react to the car," I lied.

He shot up from his chair upon seeing mom's car round the corner. "They're here!"

With his response I stood up too and followed him down the sidewalk. He threw his arms out welcoming them as they pulled in the driveway. I hung back to watch their reaction. It was at that moment that I also realized I was almost forty years old, and I still depended on my parents for help. Now a blubbering mess, the tears made rivers down my cheeks.

Chapter Sixteen

My parents decided to stay through the weekend. It was the longest planned visit they'd made since the girls were in elementary school. I was anticipating what normally came with their stay, but my four-day limit for patience was now two days late. The cycle was always the same. We would start out with hugs and kisses, love and tears of happiness at seeing everyone again. It would slowly turn into complaints about household upkeep and parenting advice, and by the fourth day I would be helping them pack their trunk and then downing a glass of wine on the front porch as I waved them out of sight trying to calm my frazzled nerves.

This time was different though. I was waiting for the fight, the disagreements on what to make for dinner or how I dealt with the pet fur on the carpet. With luck I even avoided any additional conversations about finances with my dad and lack of romance with my mom. I was actually glad they decided to extend their visit.

Saturday evening both girls surprised me when they decided to stay in to spend time with their grandparents. I looked around taking in the peaceful surroundings. My heart warmed as we settled into the living room to watch a movie. I noticed my mom staring at a spot on the wall. I turned to look, and there was nothing there. I looked back and she rolled her eyes and blinked rapidly trying to clear her mind.

"Mom? You okay?" I asked.

She looked at me. "Of course. Why?"

"Are you tired?" I answered her with another question.

"No. What's with the questions?"

"Mom! I'm just concerned. You're acting weird."

My mother turned away from me and with a deep sigh began

rocking in the chair. I looked at dad, and he just shrugged his shoulders.

As the movie began I made an assembly line for popcorn in the kitchen. One bag into the microwave, one bowl out, one new bag open, take the first bag out, repeat. As I was taking the second bag out of the microwave I turned to see my dad standing by the bar.

"That's not unusual you know," he said.

I just waited knowing he'd explain his comment.

"She stares a lot. And that thing she does with her eyes… makes me think she needs new glasses."

"You should take her to the eye doctor then." I poured the steamy popcorn into bowl #2.

"She said she went. That there was nothing wrong with her prescription."

"Dad, you are retired now. You go with her to the doctor. She goes with you. One of you is always the other set of ears in case someone doesn't hear or misunderstands—that's the rules when you are retired."

"Rules of retirement," he repeated. "I never got that guidebook."

I handed him a bowl to carry. "Well now you know. Next time, you go too, okay?"

"Noted." He nodded in agreement and followed me back to the living room. He thought I didn't see him, but he was shaking his head and laughing behind my back.

Chapter Seventeen

The next day Kennedy spent the morning trying to talk her grandparents into waiting three more days to leave.

"But you've never been to one of my lacrosse games before, and what could you possibly have to do at the house?" she pleaded.

"True. And I've always wanted to know what that odd named sport was all about," her grandpa replied. "But I'm overdue at the dentist, and if I miss one more appointment I think he'll disown me as a patient."

Kennedy turned to me. "Mom? Help me out!"

I just looked at her and shrugged my shoulders.

After she didn't move, I answered. "I can't make them stay. They are grown adults. They have things to do. I can't ask them to change appointments. We'll send them a video, okay?" Secretly, I was okay with finally having my kitchen, parenting skills, and sanity safe before arguments began.

She sulked and eventually gave up, but only because she had the part of me in her that knew fighting with that man was always a losing battle.

After twenty minutes of hugs, kisses, packing the car, repacking, explaining the best way back to the highway, drawing directions, and finally just letting dad *wing it*, I shut his door and threw up a final wave in their direction as the taillights left the driveway.

The girls had already said their goodbyes in the house. Both claimed to have homework to do before school the next day. As a mom I knew there were two things wrong with that excuse. One: no teenager did homework on a Sunday morning, and two: no teenager did homework on a Sunday period. Instead, I knew Kennedy didn't want to cry in front of them, and Presley would rather hide out in her room then be asked to help load the car.

I wasn't in the mood for arguing or calming anyone down. What I really needed was a stiff drink. My coffee would have to suffice. I took a long, loud sip and even smacked my lips into an *ahhh*. "I've been waiting all week to do that mom," I said to myself.

Chapter Eighteen

Two weeks later we finally got the first call on someone wanting to look at the house. It was 8:30 in the morning, and they would be there that afternoon. My day of grocery shopping plans would be delayed. I needed to clean the house and needed to do it fast. The girls were out for spring break, and they would also be redirected in their plans. I knew Kennedy's practice wouldn't be until 4:00 and this time we'd all be there. While practice would be going on I'd be praying for a miracle that the house would sell.

From what Bonnie told me, the couple was coming from out of town, actually driving over two hours to get here. She didn't want to sound too encouraging, but usually those kinds of people came with purpose and rarely left without putting in a contract. Regardless, my fingers would remain crossed until I heard news either way.

Presley was first to emerge into the kitchen. She was scooting her slippered feet and carrying Luke under one arm. "He's got to quit waking me up," she said with sleep in her voice.

"It's a beautiful day out there, and we have a lot to do," I said, pushing a small plate of toast and grape jam in her direction.

She pushed it back and laid her head on the table. "Just coffee please."

"Here." This time orange juice was moved in front of her.

"Ashley wanted to go to the mall today," she said with one hand on the glass and the other under her head.

"Then tell her you'll go tomorrow. We have a house to clean immaculately today. We have potential buyers coming!"

She finally lifted her head and took a drink realizing mid-sip that it wasn't coffee at all. "Uggh… coffee Mom, not juice!"

"Sorry child, I had the last cup. And yes, we have the first people coming to look at this house, and it needs to look better than this." My arm swung wide to show the things out of place.

"We are far from messy people, Mom. What do you want us to do, make it look like we don't even live here?"

I thought about that for a second. "No. Just that the people who live here are way more organized."

As Presley was leaving the room, I stopped her. "On your way to your room, tell your sister that the breakfast cart is pulling out of the kitchen in five minutes. Either she wants the toast or Luke gets it." Hearing his name the dog danced around and sat perking his ears at attention.

Chapter Nineteen

The laundry basket was overflowing from hampers I emptied as I crossed the hall from bedroom to bedroom. By the time I got to Kennedy's door I had to set it down for a better grip. I heard talking from the other side, and I leaned in to listen.

"I know, right? I can't wait," Presley said in her giddy voice.

"Only a few months and it's another summer at the beach. This time we can drive. We can be on the sand all day every day if we want," Kennedy added, and both she and Presley giggled like little girls.

I continued my journey down the stairs this time dragging the basket and thumping it on every step on the way down. It was hard to believe the girls were in fact old enough to drive, and family vacations to the beach would be different now since they didn't depend on my driving to get there. We lived so close to the ocean that within fifteen minutes we could see the coast line at Wellington Beach. As a bird flies we'd be there in half that time. Traffic around the beach area was always the worst part of the drive.

As I was throwing the last towel into the washing machine I realized that, after the house sold and the chaos calmed, we were all going to need a vacation, and the beach sounded perfect, traffic and all.

That last load of laundry was the final step in cleaning the house. The girls must have sensed the urgency to go, because they both stood in the living room waiting for me to finish. Kennedy was dressed for practice with no makeup and hair piled on top of her head in a messy bun. Presley was her usual self, ready for a date with a prince in case she ran into one. I just shook my head. No need to say it aloud. Standing before me was the picture of how opposite identical twins could be.

Chapter Twenty

"You're lying!" I screamed into the phone.

"Whoa, don't yell at me, sister." Bonnie said inches away from the receiver after I deafened her.

"I'm sorry, sorry, so sorry," I apologized.

"And no, I don't lie. You know me better than that," Bonnie continued, laughing. "Full offer price. And because his new job starts in a month they want to push this one to close quickly."

I was in shock. I found myself blindly walking toward the couch and easing onto the cushion. I made myself speak. "Wow… that's… I'm… It's just…"

"Awesome! I know. Right?"

"Fast," I answered.

I was blinking a million miles an hour like it would help absorb the information into my brain. I kind of felt like throwing up. Or passing out. I immediately knew I had to get off the phone in case either or both happened.

"I'll call you later Bonnie."

"Sounds good," she said with too much excitement.

For some reason my mouth wouldn't move and no *good-bye* or *okay* could be said, so instead I just pushed the off button.

I sat in silence for the better part of an hour. I felt like I was dreaming, but my continuous blinking made me realize I was wide awake. After deciding that I had too much planning to do to waste it staring into space, I called Bonnie back.

"And don't worry, the house you liked is still available, and in fact it's vacant. So you'll have a place to live," she encouraged.

I laughed. "Good. You know I was worried."

"Have you calmed down?"

"No."

"Yes you have. You know you're excited."

I gave in. "Yes, I am. I'm more afraid of the girls' reactions."

"They will be fine, Pam. And remind them that the new house is closer to the beach. All girls want that."

I thanked her and arranged to sign paperwork the next day. By then she hoped to have a better idea for a closing date.

Chapter Twenty-One

After talking with Bonnie, the next day I determined the final closing date she estimated would be during the week of the girls' junior trip to New York. I silently said a prayer that they'd be gone while all the chaos with moving would be going on at the house. Only one of us needed that stress.

While Presley and Kennedy were at school I began to plan the packing. I toted boxes to their room and stacked them in clear corners. We had long ago downsized, and my estimated six boxes each would be plenty. Most of the clothes and toiletries would be bagged and transported by car. I wanted them to be very convenient so there could be no complaints on finding anything for school. The girls were already mad about the move. They were just now getting use to the fact that it was going to happen and that we would all be better off. Well, maybe they weren't quite ready to hear the *we'd be better off* part, but they did understand that the only way to stay in this house is to be adopted by the new couple who would be moving in.

On my way back downstairs the phone rang. Kicking boxes out of the way I made it on the final ring. Before I could say hello, Bonnie was already talking.

"So, I arranged for you to go look at the other house tomorrow afternoon. How does that sound?"

"Great," I answered bending down to clean up the mess of dog food that spilled when the kicked boxes flew across the floor. Both dogs were already helping by eating every stray piece they could find.

As I wondered why they decided that *now* was the time they had to eat the food that had been there all morning, Bonnie continued talking. "We have as much time as you need because there's nobody in there. And now I want you to really inspect everything, okay? I want to know all the issues you might have so we can go into battle. These people already moved away so they're willing to deal. They want to sell this house yesterday. Don't just go in there and give the asking price like your guys did. We need to make a plan. I just—"

"Okay, okay… geez," I stopped her. "You need to take a breath sometime, you know!"

Bonnie apologized. "I'm sorry. I'm just so happy for you. This is exciting, and I love my job, don't get me wrong, but when it's this personal it means so much more."

As she talked more about the property we would be visiting the next day and about the process and the paperwork involved in the closing, I moved boxes into other rooms. While cradling the phone on my chin I answered and agreed where necessary, but after fifteen minutes of sacrificing the use of my neck I told her I had to go and that I would meet her at the office at noon the next day.

Just as I laid my phone on the bar it rang again. Thinking Bonnie was calling back again to give me more information on the closing, I blindly answered the phone, not bothering to check caller ID. "What did you forget this time?"

"Pammy?" It was my dad.

"Dad! Wow… I'm sorry… I thought…" I was startled into realization of the new caller. Then I immediately wondered why he used the name, *Pammy*. He only used that when he's concerned about something, like when he did when I was upset on the porch when they visited.

I didn't have time to ask before he continued, "Pammy… it's your mom. She's had a seizure. It's not good. We're at the hospital."

Chapter Twenty-Two

"I'm sorry. You're just going to have to miss school tomorrow," I said, as I shuffled the overnight bags out the front door.

"But moooommm…"

It's amazing how many syllables that little word can be made into.

"The girls on the squad are meeting to discuss plans for summer dance camp. I need to be there. I mean, what are they gonna think if I'm not there, and I want to try out for captain?" Presley argued.

She would make a good lawyer one day, or an actress. Either way she would make a good living, I thought.

"Gran needs us right now. We're going to the hospital, and by we, I mean the whole family. You included." I shut the door behind her before she could escape back inside. Kennedy was already in the car, just excited to play hooky for a day. I could see her on the cell phone and knew she was talking with her grandpa.

We rode in silence through the neighborhood, and I finally asked Kennedy for an update from Dad. "He said she's awake now but in a lot of pain. Apparently she hit both her head and right arm when she fell. They think her wrist might even be fractured."

I silently said a prayer that she would be okay. Presley grunted her concern.

"Dad said she was in the kitchen when it happened. She must have hit the tile floor," I explained.

Beside me, Kennedy made a gasp as if she felt the pain. Presley again grunted from the backseat.

I gave her a look in the rearview mirror, but after trying to hold back I found that I couldn't. "Presley, it's only one meeting. One day. If the team can't understand that you are needed elsewhere and that this is a *family* emergency you don't have much of a relationship with them, now do you?"

She just stared back in response and mouthed *okay*.

What? No grunt and an actual word? I saw progress being made. We were getting better at this communication thing.

Chapter Twenty-Three

King Lake is located on the outskirts of the Jefferson National Forest in Western Virginia. It's a scenic area with trees blooming and green grass as far as the eye can see. The countryside and mountains are breathtaking, beautiful, and exhilarating. The eight-hour trip to get there is none of those things.

Reasoning behind the demise of the road trip fell in a few different faults; all of which were mine I'm sure. First, taking two very hyper dogs on a long trip is never a fun adventure for anyone. They made it very clear that they ruled the car. Second, I let the girls take turns driving. There were fights over who drove the longest amount of time, who had the best technique, and who fairly kept the dogs from jumping on the other's lap. Finally, and most importantly, the mistake was made of not explaining that it does, in fact, take the full eight hours to get there. No magic jet was secretly built into the trunk of my sedan.

So by the time we pulled up to my mom and dad's house we were all tired of the drive and tired of each other. Visiting hours at the hospital had ended. Having just pulled into the driveway ahead of us, Dad was walking toward the house. He looked tired but managed hardy hugs all around. The girls walked ahead of him into the house, and he stayed behind with me in the entryway to give an update.

"She's okay. Just sore," he said.

"What happened? And why?" I asked.

"I really don't know. I heard a terrible crash in the kitchen and came running. By the time I got there she was in a full grand mal seizure. It was awful. I couldn't dial 911 quick enough. My hands were shaking." Abruptly, he grew quiet.

"Do they know what caused it?"

He shook his head before answering. "They're still running tests. They have some scans scheduled for tomorrow. We'll know more then I guess."

I sank into the chair in the entry way behind me and stared into the living room where the girls had found the remote and turned on a reality show.

"If it's something that was reoccurring, or that's been affecting her for a while… I… I just don't understand what signs could have been missed." He sighed. "I don't know."

Suddenly, it hit me. The staring that I was doing now was similar to what mom did when she was visiting. And that blinking that she did as if trying to focus. I stood up. "What if how she was acting when you guys were at the house—you know, the blinking, her staring—what if it was… was a sign?"

"I thought the same thing as soon as it happened. I even told the doctors, and they're using that information to figure everything out too. Pam, it's okay. She's in good hands. If there is something wrong they'll find it."

I looked at him. "It doesn't matter. We never would have thought something like this would have happen."

He came to my side and put his hand on my shoulder. I turned to him for a hug, and he spoke into my hair. "She'll be fine. You know she's too stubborn to ever leave me on my own."

Unfortunately those were famous last words for many people. I squeezed my eyes shut praying for mom, who I now realized I needed to have more in my life now than I ever thought I did; nagging, stubbornness, critiquing of parenting skills and all.

Chapter Twenty-Four

The doctor arrived for rounds as early as we did the next morning. I caught him at the nurse's station on my way to find Mom's room.

"You're looking for Ms. Taylor?" He looked up from the chart and over reading glasses that were perched on the front of his nose. "She's actually my patient."

I looked up at him in question. His sandy brown hair and contrasting deep blue eyes were an odd combination. He looked too young for reading glasses but wise enough with some years of age. I found it difficult to keep from looking at him. It wasn't that he was drop dead muscle-laden gorgeous—he was instead attractive in a subdued, reserved way. The way he looked back at me made me think he was hurried or shy.

"I'm sorry. I'm Dr. Hamilton, her neurologist." He held out his hand to shake.

I took it and after a few seconds found my voice. "I'm Pam Taylor, her daughter. How is she?"

He turned to give me his full attention before answering. "She's had a good night, rested well; but she has a busy morning ahead of her. Some scans are scheduled for the next couple hours. By lunchtime we may have a better answer as to why this happened."

"Thank you, doctor," I said wanting to say more but losing my thought once again.

"I'll let you know as soon as we're done. You still have about forty-five minutes before she's taken down if you want to visit," he added as he turned to walk from the counter.

"Thank you again… Doctor." I quietly said, turning toward her room so he wouldn't see my face turning red.

I thought about Dr. Hamilton as I walked down the hall. I

looked back at the nurse's station to see if anyone else grew as embarrassed to talk to him as I did. Nobody acted like it. For all I knew he really wasn't considered good looking. He could have had four eyes and a cow's head, but nonetheless he was a guy, and it had been a while since I was that close and personal to one. In fact, it had been a very, very long time since I had contact with a man, let alone even a brief and non-intrusive conversation as I just had. No wonder I found him so attractive.

Even if my perception of beauty was correct, he was probably happily married with five kids anyway. The whole situation just made me think that maybe it was time to start testing the waters again. Moving and the kids becoming seniors soon and all the other changes could mean another one was needed too, with my love life. If the kids could do it, why couldn't I? Yeah, why not?

Brought back to reality, I remembered. There, lying in the hospital bed was Mom.

That was why not.

Chapter Twenty-Five

Her right arm was in a brace. She was aggressively changing channels with her free left one when I walked in her room. She didn't even look over at who had entered before she loudly commented. "You'd think in this day and age we could get some decent channels."

I exaggerated a sigh as I came around the curtain.

"Pam, my darling!" She held out her arms.

When I reached for a light hug, careful not to tangle all the wires and tubes attached to her, she immediately asked why I was there.

"Well Mom, you—that's why! You're in the hospital. You had a seizure. Why wouldn't I be here?"

"I don't know. You live the whole way across the state. And we were just there visiting," she answered with thicker sarcasm than usual.

I bit my tongue reminding myself that she was in the hospital. She might be very sick. I had to filter the words that I said next.

"I talked with Dr. Hamilton. He was at the nurse's station."

She looked at me over the rim of her glasses. "Who's Dr. Hamilton?"

"He's your neurologist, Mom. He saw you this morning."

"Well I didn't hear his name when he came in. I know who you're talking about. He just talked on and on about tests and scans and such."

I walked to the window, noting that the bright early sun should lighten her mood. "He actually seemed very nice, determined even to find out what's wrong with you."

She just grunted deeply in response. I knew now where Presley got it from.

I turned around and glared at her. "Mom. We all want to help you. I know you don't like being here. Do you really think I couldn't be doing a million other things right now? I have a house to pack. Dad would rather be at home, watching something about history on television or building another shelf or cabinet for your shoes or books. But I dropped everything. He dropped everything. Your health is more important to us than that. We are all here because we care. About you."

"There is nothing wrong with me. I'm fine. You should have saved your gas money. And your dad doesn't have to be here with me. I can just call him for a ride when they release me."

"Okay. Well, I'll be back in a little while." I shook my head and turned, walking back to the waiting room. Why was it that the woman couldn't accept a gift, wouldn't take a free compliment, and argued for the sake of arguing even to inanimate objects like the poor television?

Chapter Twenty-Six

 D ad was in the waiting room with the girls when I walked in. "Wow, that wasn't even fifteen minutes," he said in a questioning tone as if to imply the visit didn't go well.

"Just wanted to make sure you got to see her before she was taken down. The doctor said they'd be coming any minute," I lied.

Instead of asking questions, he stood up to take his turn. He could always handle her better anyway.

Since his leaving the room, I had been paging through a magazine pretending to read and barely noticing the pictures on the pages. Across the room, Presley and Kennedy were curled in chairs and engrossed in listening to their music with earbuds in a corner.

I rolled my head around on my neck relieving tension while focusing on the television that hung in the middle of the wall. The sound was muted but I could tell disturbing news was being described. The anchors' faces were tense, and the images of smoke and fire appeared moments later. I watched the silent screen for a while trying to figure out what was being said. I never understood why there were televisions in the hospital that continually played depressing news stories, or why the sound was never turned up. It's like they wanted to remind you why you were there but not upset you too much by making you listen to it. After just a few minutes I scowled and shook my head as if answering my own thoughts. I went back to leafing through the magazine. The coffee pot *clicked* shutting off to my right.

Although the three of us were the only ones in the room, Presley and Kennedy still sat in silence in the corner. I assumed they were still upset about this unplanned adventure we were on, and I knew better than to ask if they wanted to see mom. Doing so would have been as disturbing as asking them to trade their clothes or shoes with strangers on the street. I decided one last cup of coffee before the pot went cold was required in order to survive the rest of the morning.

Chapter Twenty-Seven

Dad walked back into the room as I was finishing my latest and last cup of caffeine. I looked at him out of the side of my eye and could see he was concerned.

"They just took her down."

I nodded before speaking. "Did they say how long it would be?"

"They didn't know, said they'd come get us when she was done."

Kennedy had pulled out her ear buds to listen. I patted the seat beside me as a silent motion for her to join us.

As she sank into the low seat to my right he continued. "I'm just scared. I'm scared they'll find something. I'm scared they won't... and then what do we do?"

"They'll just keep looking," Kennedy spoke up for the first time that morning.

"That's right," I agreed. "Doctors don't just throw the towel in anymore, and when they find something, they fix it."

Across the room and unaware to any of us, Presley had turned off her music as well. "It's because doctors want to collect more money. More tests, more money. Having an excuse to fix something... well that's more money too. It's really all about the money," she said.

I gave her a stare telling her that it was not the right time for her opinion about the healthcare system. Another reason, though, she confirmed my idea that politics might just be the best arena for her college education.

I turned sideways to face my dad. I needed to have *the talk* with him that no child wanted to have. "Dad. Have you thought about what will happen if... well... if something happens to mom?"

He knew what I implied. His brow narrowed with concern and

it took him a few seconds to answer. "No… and I don't want to. I know I don't think I'd survive."

"Do you have a will? Emergency plans? Anything?"

He just sat there. I didn't know if that meant yes, no, maybe, or all of the above.

"Well, if you don't have it we've got to get something in place. What if they find something they can't fix?"

"Don't talk like that, Mom," Kennedy whispered in exasperation.

"We *are* here for a reason," I whispered back then continued out loud but rhetorically to myself. "I just can't believe you two haven't already made decisions. How can you go through an entire lifetime of marriage and not know what will happen if you die before your spouse?"

Dad hung his head. "We didn't think we'd need to. Or, maybe we've known we needed to but it's something you just put off… until you need it." Sighing deeply he continued, "But you're right. You made your point. I just don't want to talk about it anymore, not right now."

The way he said it made me regret how harsh I came across. I had forgotten that I was his only support at the moment and that I needed to be there for him while we waited. There were two chairs between us and I quickly moved to the one directly beside him. I hugged him and whispered my love and that I was there for him and always would be. Seconds later I felt one and then a second set of arms encircle us as the girls joined in showing their affection as well. Instantly, my eyes welled with tears and my heart ached with love.

Chapter Twenty-Eight

Tumor? I tried to understand what Dr. Hamilton was saying. He had a glum look on his face when he entered the room and delivered the news.

Dad sat beside me speechless. Mom gasped at the word from the bed to his left.

I was the first to speak up. "Tumor? As in cancer?"

The doctor firmly shook his head. "No, not cancer—just tumor. In fact, tumors."

"There is more than one in my head?" Mom's eyes grew twice their normal size, and her mouth remained hanging open after asking.

He went on to explain his findings. "You have two masses, side by side, touching if you will, and total about the size of a marble. They are pressing on the temporal lobe of the brain—this area right here." He pointed to the left side of his head.

I appreciated the fact that he used layman terms for the common people that we were. He wasn't the kind of doctor to start with the medical jargon, confusing a person, and then explaining everything all over again making it seem like the patient was an imbecile.

"But they aren't cancerous?" my dad spoke up.

"I don't think so." He stopped himself before sounding unsure. "What I mean is that everything we've done with testing so far shows that they are not cancerous. Once we remove them, we'll send them to the path lab for a more detailed examination."

My mom sighed deeply, sounding defeated. "So when will we be scheduling surgery?"

"Oh, it's already scheduled," he replied as he glanced at his watch. Bright and early. Six A.M. tomorrow, so… roughly thirteen hours from now."

As if on cue a petite middle-aged female doctor walked into the room. She was cradling a chart under her arm and extended her small cold hand before reaching the end of the bed. I took it before the introduction was even made.

"I'm Dr. Bryson. I'll be the surgeon."

"Wait, what about Dr. Hamilton." I stopped mid-shake and looked over at him.

Before she could say anything, he explained. "Don't worry. I'll be there too. But you'll want Dr. Bryson to lead the surgery team. She's the Head of Neurosurgery here at Western General."

We all looked at her. I forced a smile and hoped Mom and Dad did the same. Then I asked about the length of time the surgery would take, the needed information remaining, and possible complications. My dad sat in silence but listened intently.

My mom appeared to be in shock.

Dr. Bryson sat at the foot of the bed and directed her answers to my mom. "First, I want you to know I'm going to take very good care of you. We have planned for the surgery to take between five to six hours. In all honesty, it probably won't take that long. And as far as complications… we feel confident we will be able to get everything while we're in there. The surface seems to be smooth enough, and the walls aren't attached to any vital tissue. This should be easy for all of us." She paused reassuringly, looking at everyone's faces.

"Once we ensure the masses are completely removed, we can get a better idea of what will come in way of recovery. Two major concerns we do have are prolonged speech difficulties and memory problems. It's believed that the surgery to remove the tumors will decrease these effects. Also, the tumors are lying extremely close to the auditory nerve of the ear. We want to make sure full function of hearing remains. After recovery you will be set up in a room on the ICU floor for a night or two. Then you'll be moved to a regular room for four to six more days. That completely depends on recovery time. Everyone is different. Those are just averages we've seen."

She looked again at everyone before asking. "Anymore questions, before I leave?"

We all shook our heads in silence.

"Okay then," she said getting up, "I'll see you in the morning."

After she left the room, Dr. Hamilton explained that a few more people would be visiting the room—the anesthesiologist, a representative from surgical admitting, and someone from the lab to draw blood would all be there before the night was over.

Looking at Mom's arm in the brace, I silently thanked the Lord that at least it wasn't broken. But after listening to the doctor talk about more tests, more visitors, and less sleep, I couldn't help but think it all sounded like a night at the zoo with a full moon.

Chapter Twenty-Nine

I had to break the news to the girls. After the conversation with doctors Hamilton and Bryson the trip home would have to be delayed. They would miss another day of school. And worse, I'd have another day of sulking girls to tend to.

The good news was that I convinced myself no matter what, praying all went well with the surgery of course, I would have them back at school on Tuesday in time for Kennedy's next lacrosse game and Presley's second meeting about dance camp.

After gathering strength for the confrontation I'd face with the girls, I left Dr. Hamilton to say his goodbyes to my parents while I tracked down Kennedy and Presley. I found them at the vending machines outside the waiting area.

They turned around in unison when they heard my footsteps approaching. "What did the doctor say?" Kennedy asked.

I briefly explained what was found and the impending surgery that would follow. Each looked concerned and then disappointed when I told them the news about not leaving until Monday.

It surprised me when Presley was the one to speak up. "It's okay mom. I think we need to be here for the surgery."

I knew it was probably not without an ulterior motive that she wanted to stay, but I was too exhausted to play detective. I encircled her shoulders and kissed her head. I pulled Kennedy close and did the same for her.

"And it's just one more day I won't have to give my speech to the class," Presley added.

There it was; the hidden truth was exposed. No detective work needed.

Chapter Thirty

I would have had a panic attack sometime during the following day if I had time in my schedule to do so. And I'm glad breathing is a natural reflex, or I'd have been in the ICU beside mom.

The surgery went great. It took four and a half hours, less than what they planned which made me worry that it went too well. Being the only four people waiting for news from the surgical suites, we had set up shop in the ICU waiting room. My dad and I were passing each other while pacing the floor when Dr. Hamilton walked in with his surgical scarf still on his head.

"Ed. Pam. Went great guys." He smiled before continuing. "We've already sent the tumors to pathology. We won't probably get a full report back for a few days, but I've asked to be immediately notified when they have the results. Once Janice wakes and has been transferred out of recovery, we'll let you know, and you can take turns visiting. At that time we'll also see if there are any residual effects from the surgery."

Dad and I each took turns shaking the doctor's hand, and he quietly shut the door behind him as he left the room. I took a deep breath and Dad simply looked at me with his lips pursed.

"And again we wait," Presley said looking up from a teen magazine she'd bought from the gift shop.

Chapter Thirty-One

The shining sun was so crisp and bright that morning of the surgery. The crystal-clear view outside was amazingly brilliant. I believed God was with us in that waiting room and gave us the perfect view to sooth our souls.

But by the time we got the okay to visit Mom, the sun had been blanketed with dark gray clouds, and a strong breeze was picking up. A strange chill ran down my spine, as if preparing me for the worst.

I shook the feeling off and reminded myself everything would be fine. The worst part was being on the road driving through the approaching bad weather.

Mom was groggy, and her head was bandaged with thick padding on the left side making it appear to be grotesquely lopsided. When I took my turn in the room, she talked very little but thanked me for being there and told me she loved me. There was a slight slur to her speech, but I didn't know if that was just from the anesthesia or one of the lasting effects the doctor talked about. Regardless, she was okay. The tumor was gone. And she remembered me. Even if the slurred speech was permanent, she was alive and tumor free.

The most she stayed awake for was five to ten minutes at a time. She would nod off, mouth hanging open, and after she drifted off for the third time, I kissed her forehead, told her I would see her soon, and went to gather the girls for the long ride home. I knew it wouldn't matter if I stayed longer or not. She was going to probably be like that for the rest of the day at least. My dad would call if something changed.

Before leaving, I hugged him tightly and stayed in his embrace for an extra moment. I whispered my love and asked that he take care of her but to call if anything changed.

"Let me tie up loose ends and take care of my house. Then, I will try to get back here soon," I said.

He nodded and a look of need flashed over his eyes.

"I will, okay?"

He mouthed his goodbye and quickly hugged the girls. We gathered our luggage and the pups from their house and were on the road just after one o'clock. I knew that with traffic slowed from the rain and the change in time we'd probably be there after eleven. I arched by back and sank comfortably into the seat for the long road ahead.

Chapter Thirty-Two

Not an hour into the drive we were sideswiped by a truck pulling an enclosed trailer. He caught my driver's side door and mirror. Thank goodness the girls were on the opposite side. I held my anger in while in front of the policeman as we stood in the rain and exchanged insurance information.

By the time I was back in the car, I was shaking from both the cool rain that now soaked through my jacket as well as the fact that I didn't have time for a person's selfish driving decisions.

And my poor car. I was quickly becoming deflated.

The clock read 11:06 when we pulled into the driveway. Tired, the girls quietly walked side by side like zombies into the house, their gait in sync. Even the sway of their hair rocked in the same direction. As I was standing on the sidewalk letting the dogs out, I could see their bedroom lights turn off virtually simultaneously.

I guess sometimes they can be alike.

<h1 style="text-align:center">Chapter Thirty-Three</h1>

No news was good news, right? As I stared out the window at the rising sun I waited for my dad to call. I slept with the phone, on the couch, in my shoes. I'm not sure why. Even if he called with an emergency, I was still a day's drive away from the hospital. I wasn't going to run there.

The girls quietly came downstairs, ate breakfast in silence, and stumbled out the door with only a quick hug and an 'I love you' apiece. I knew they were tired. I hoped their school day wouldn't be affected by the trip.

Soon after they left I dialed the hospital to talk with someone. Dad. The doctor. A nurse. Anyone who had an update on my mom.

Dad reassured me. "Pam, it's okay. She slept all day yesterday after you left. There was nothing to call and tell you about."

"And last night? This morning?" I asked.

"She's still foggy. They said it could be a little while until she's fully aware, and with the pain medicine she'll probably be out of it even longer."

"When you know something, call me. And I'm going to check back later. So you'd better call me before then. Or I'll worry. Please don't make me worry."

At noon I was tracking down Dr. Hamilton. I had already been transferred around the nurse's station. Everyone was passive with what was said and careful with words. I knew Dad wouldn't ask the right questions either, so I was out of options. I should have stayed there. I was kicking myself now as I paced the floor.

When Dr. Hamilton got on the line, he explained. "I'm concerned with certain aspects of her memory. It could be the swelling. There is no need for immediate concern. We'll only know more over time.

She's asked for more pain medication. I upped the dose just a bit. I'm afraid she'll use it as a crutch… a way to disguise these lapses in memory if she relies on just sleeping it away. Does that make sense? I know it's a lot to take in, but…"

I wanted to reach through the phone and hug him. It was the most information I had gotten from anyone.

"How long will she be in the hospital?" I kept my quick pace around the room.

"As it stands now, she'll probably be here until the end of the week. She might be able to go home by this weekend at the earliest. If all goes well she'll be downgraded in a few days and moved to a room on the general patient floor for the remainder of her stay."

I noted that his voice expressed genuine concern, and I didn't know many doctors that spent so much time explaining a medical situation as he had. He was a godsend for mom.

"Please tell her, if she's able to understand, that I will be there again this weekend. I will be with her when she comes home."

"She'll like that," he replied with smile in his voice.

Chapter Thirty-Four

It was Presley who came to talk to me that afternoon. I was robotically packing and cleaning my bedroom when she walked into the room and sat down on the bed beside me.

"Are you okay, Mom?" she asked. "I mean. I know you're sad and worried but do you want to talk about it?"

I smiled thinking how she really had listened all those times I gave the *mom speech*. "Pres, honey, I'm fine, just stressed. I have so much on my plate and no appetite to eat."

She looked at me, amused with my analogy.

"What I mean is, I'm being pulled in so many directions with so much going on. It's hard not to just jump off the St. John Bridge. And as much as I do, it doesn't seem like enough."

"Gran will be fine. She has Pap, and when we can, we'll go back." Presley leaned in with a hug.

I wrapped my arms around her pulling her tight to me. It was so rare that she allowed me to get this close to her that I wanted to lose myself in the moment. Through her hair I blushed and stifled a laugh. Sometimes a parent needs parenting, even by her child.

As we pulled away I lightened the mood with teenager talk. There were only moments I was given with this girl, especially when she was willing to talk, and I was going to take complete advantage of it.

"So where is Kennedy? It's early. I didn't think she had practice yet."

"She was going to get ice cream with Mike."

I sat back. "Mike? What happened to Jake? Who's Mike?"

She stood up, and I could tell I was entering a no-parent zone.

"Jake *was* Kennedy's boyfriend, but he liked me. That wasn't gonna happen though. I like Mark."

"So where's Jake now?"

"I don't know, but Kennedy actually wants to go out with Matt."

"Who?"

"Matt… You know, Matt, down the street."

"Not Mike?" Wait, did you say you like a Mark?

"Mom!"

I fell back onto the mattress. "I'm tired. My head hurts. I need a nap."

Chapter Thirty-Five

Having no hours at work, I finished most of the packing throughout the rest of the week. By Thursday evening I only lacked the furniture. I decided living out of a couple laundry baskets and totes would have to suffice, because once the bags and boxes were being filled I didn't want to leave any space. That included emptying the dressers, closets, and kitchen cabinets. Each room had one or two totes or baskets labeled with the name of that room. If you couldn't find it in them you didn't need to use it until after moving day. I know it was too soon for most of the packing, but I honestly didn't know where I'd be between my parents and the old and new houses. Speaking of, I still hadn't heard anything from Bonnie about the new house. I called her, but she wasn't in. I left a message for her to call back.

My cell phone vibrated just as I was carrying down the last load from upstairs. "Your mom's been transferred to the general floor… finally," my dad said on the other line. I could hear the tiredness coating his voice.

"You don't sound happy," I said.

"I'm just glad we made some progress. I never thought we'd get the green light. I was hoping to be home this weekend. Now… well, now I don't know when it will be." He sounded defeated.

"I'm sure the doctor has great hope that it will be soon."

"Ha, *hope*. Seems it certainly isn't an outlook for improvement."

"Why do you say that, Dad?"

He sighed, and I could hear him shuffle around the room. I guessed he was walking into the hallway for privacy. "It's just that he talks about the long road ahead, but there aren't any definites, heck not even estimates."

"Dad, why would he tell you something that he doesn't even know? We all hope for the best. Doctors just hope for no bad surprises and an accurate diagnosis."

He sat in silence, and before I could think my mouth opened and the words poured out. "I'm coming back there tomorrow for the weekend. You need a break, and I need to see my mom".

My call waiting told me Bonnie was calling back. I said my goodbyes before he could argue and then I clicked over the line.

"Hey girl… I got your message. I'm sorry we haven't gotten over to see that house. I just didn't know if you wanted to be bothered yet," she said before I even said hello.

"It's okay. I need to hold off until next week, but I have a question for you."

Bonnie reminded me that the house has been on the market for so long that she doubted anyone would find it until then. "And what can I do for you?"

"Would you mind if the pups and girls stayed over there for the weekend? I know they don't want to do the cross-state traveling again anytime soon, but I really need to be there for Mom."

She didn't hesitate, and in a way I could tell she was excited to help. "Of course! You know those girls are like my own. I'll get the spare room made up this evening."

"Thanks Bonnie. And I really hope my life calms down soon."

"For your sake and mine… me too." She laughed.

Chapter Thirty-Six

Just as I arrived on the outskirts of King Lake, an odd feeling came over me. I began to panic, almost scream out as if I was in pain. I had turned the radio off miles before, just using my thoughts to keep me company. But as the hospital came into view, I knew my mom needed me at that moment.

The car was barely in park when I jumped out pulling my purse by the strap and sprinting up the cement stairs into the visitor's entrance. The receptionist started to stand and greet me before noticing my concerned expression and just sank back into her chair. I was rapidly punching the elevator button seconds later, pacing as I waited for it to arrive.

Dad was walking out of her room as I rounded the corner and hurried down the hall. We collided just as he turned his head to look in my direction. He grabbed my forearms before speaking. "Whoa pumpkin, you were sure in a hurry to get here. Heck, it seems like just a few hours ago we were talking as you left the house."

I explained the odd anxiety I felt as I got closer to the hospital and was interrupted by Mom's voice. "Pam, is that you?"

I peeked around the door frame and saw her sitting up in bed, newly bathed and dressed, and almost the same as before the surgery.

"Mom! You… you're okay!?" It came out more of a question.

She nodded. "I feel better, yeah."

Dad came to my side and whispered that the doctor wanted to see us as soon as I got there. From his eyes I could tell there was concern he's been keeping inside.

As if on cue, I heard Dr. Hamilton's voice at the nurse's desk. I hurried out of the room to catch him, and he stopped mid-stride as he heard me call for him.

"You made it, Pam." He smiled. "Great to see you again. How was the trip?"

"Tiring. But Dad said you needed to speak with us." As much as I wanted to be, I wasn't in the mood for small talk.

As if he read my mind he pointed to a small office ahead to the right. "I'll meet you in there in five minutes, okay?"

I stood to the side, hidden from mom's view and motioned for Dad to join me in the hall. I could hear him tell mom we'd be right back, and she laughed saying she wasn't going anywhere and then she blew a kiss.

A kiss? That was my first warning flag. Giggling, shy comments? That wasn't like her. Mom normally would have argued that she couldn't stand the hospital, said something to the effect of *"get me a diet soda since I'm stuck here,"* or just grumbled in reply. I'm not saying she would be rude or mean, but happy and funny were not her normal traits.

Chapter Thirty-Seven

Brain. Damage. Really, those are the only words I heard. I know he mentioned other stuff, probably even important stuff, but as soon as he said *Brain... Damage...* he became muffled and fuzzy, and for all I know was speaking a foreign language.

Eventually he said, "Questions?"

I hoped Dad had been paying more attention than I was. I looked at him, and it was apparent he wasn't.

"So, what do we do now?" I asked.

He leaned back in his leather chair, crossed his legs, resting his ankle on his knee, and folded his hands on top. "We wait."

After I didn't say anything, he continued. "We wait and see what happens. And I know that doesn't sound like an answer. Honestly, it's not an answer. But there is nothing we can do at this moment. I have scheduled a more detailed scan of the area, but with *Brain. Damage*"—there we go again—"it's hard to pinpoint how it will affect the individual."

"But Dr. Hamilton, you've been doing this for many years. What do you *think* will happen?" I asked.

My dad jumped in. "You can't just say you don't know."

The doctor took a moment and let out a deep sigh. "Okay, in my honest opinion, I think what you see may be what you get. I don't expect to see a change for the worse, but then again I doubt it will get better either. I'm sorry I can't give a perfect answer."

The handshake he gave us when we left was sincere. I could tell he deeply felt sorry. I leaned in and gave him a hug whispering into his ear. "It's okay. I'm just glad you kept her here with us. Thank you for that."

When I pulled away, he smiled, and I could see the tears begin to rim his eyes, and he quickly excused himself claiming the need to see another patient.

When we entered Mom's room again, she was staring out the window. At first I thought, with the way her head was tilted on the pillow, that she was sleeping. When I got closer, I could see her wide eyes, blinking ever few seconds. Dad elbowed me and whispered. "She's been doing that too." That was the second sign.

I walked around to the side she was looking at and sat down on the bed bringing her focus back to me. She moved her eyes but not her head. She gave a half smile, and I patted her covered leg.

"It will all be okay, mom. We're here for you. We'll always be here for you," I softly spoke.

She cocked her head, and her eyes widened before speaking. "You look familiar. Do I know you?" she asked.

I closed my eyes.

Sign number three.

Chapter Thirty-Eight

I quickly stood in shock, staring at my mom. I wanted to cry, to scream. But I just stood there, my heart breaking.

As if someone pushed my back, willing me toward her, I moved to the bed. I slowly sat back down on the edge and gently touched her hand. She didn't move it as I thought she would, and that gave me hope. The room was now empty except for the two of us. My dad must have stepped out. The pain was probably too great for him. Slowly, as if a dimmer light switch was turned on, her eyes began to light up, and she smiled. "Pam, I love you dear. Thank you for visiting me."

I nodding, pursing my lips together hoping she could see my return of love in my eyes.

"I don't want you to go, to be so far away," she said in a very childlike voice. And before I knew it I was weeping into her chest.

I hugged her tight and told her that she was my mom, my life. "I can't go anywhere. But I can't stay." If my heart wasn't broken before, it truly shattered at that moment.

"It scares me," she said as she caressed my head with her IVed and bandaged hand.

I looked up through bleary eyes. "What does, Mom?"

"This. Everything. Forgetting things. Remembering things. Wanting to be home but not knowing what will happen when I get there. And the doctors and nurses whisper when they think I can't hear. I know what they say. It may not ever get better. It just scares me."

I sat up and paused before talking again. "It scares all of us—even the doctors and nurses—and us, your family, especially. I am here because you need me. I wish I could stay longer, but for now I'm here. I'm not going anywhere."

That night, I prayed. I realized it had been years since I was on my knees, hands folded and truly needing to talk with God. I guess I had been so blessed that I forgot to talk with Him on a regular basis. I hoped He didn't forget about me, and more importantly that He still knew my voice.

"Lord, I have a major issue on my hands. My mom needs me. My kids need me. And both are separated by so many miles. If I am truly meant to stay here give me strength. Make the move possible for us. If we are meant to be on the coast let that be known as well. My entire faith is held with You at this moment. Show me a sign… any sign. Show me the way. Thank You. Amen."

Thank you? That sounded odd. But appropriate. I guess.

Within minutes I fell asleep.

Chapter Thirty-Nine

It felt like seconds later when a continual ringing sounded. I recognized my cell phone ringer and sat up, wide awake. Mom!

"Hello." I frantically said through a raspy, sleep-covered voice.

"Oh, you were sleeping! I'm so sorry I woke you up." It was Bonnie.

"No. I mean, it's okay. What time is it?" I fought to find a clock in the guest room. Nothing. Who doesn't put a clock in a guest room?

"It's almost eight o'clock there," she answered.

"Really? Holy cow I slept late. And hard. Wow. Sorry."

"Pam. I'm so sorry to call again. But that house you wanted? That cute Cape Cod? Walker Realty down the street put a contract on it last night. Can you believe that?"

I let a chuckle out. I could actually. I got my sign. I couldn't help but smile. I knew I should have been sad. I wasn't. I was so relieved to have an answer that I told Bonnie about my prayer, about my mom and what was going on. If she was sad she didn't sound it.

"Oh Pam, I will do anything to help you."

"I'm glad you said that. Since you have sold our house… and well, we are now officially homeless… do you think we could crash at your place for a month or so, maybe use that apartment over your garage?"

She was quick to respond. "Oh yeah, of course you can. It's just sitting empty anyway. But you aren't going to want to stay there long. It's small, too sma—"

I stopped her. "No, I know that, and I would never want to put you out."

"Put me out?" Bonnie dramatically gasped. "Friends never *put* each other out. We *help* each other out. If you feel like you need to compensate me consider it payback for when you gave up your spare bedroom for us when the house was getting fumigated for termites—twice."

"Okay, I guess two nights for one room versus a few weeks for an apartment sounds about equal. Deal!" I was quick to reply knowing so much needed to be done to get the ball rolling.

It was official. We were moving to King Lake. I said a silent *Thank You*, for my sign. I knew that I would still need to stay here until my mom was better, but I couldn't uproot the girls. They only had a few weeks of school left, and I wasn't about to move them. But knowing they would have a place to stay, even if I had to be here was another blessing I hadn't even prayed about.

After hanging up with Bonnie, I quickly dressed and was heading to the hospital minutes later.

My phone rang just as I walked through the front entrance. "I'm downstairs…" I started to say to my dad when I saw who was calling.

"It's me," Mom said excitedly. "I'm going home today. Isn't that wonderful news?"

It most certainly was. I stopped at the elevator bank and stared at a poster that showed Jesus' healing hand as He touched a small child's head. The ad was for a church benefit to raise money for the pediatric ward. I thought about the answer to my prayer and the healing hand of God that I now entrusted for my mom. As she would leave the hospital, she would need more than the health care system or family could provide. We would be there for her immediate needs. The Lord would be there for her eternal needs. I smiled.

The door of the elevator opened, and a young lady walked out and saw my face. "It's such a beautiful day isn't it?" she said.

I simply responded, "Absolutely perfect."

Chapter Forty

Mom slept the entire afternoon. I think she had missed the comfort and peace of her home. Dad watched a sports channel and fell asleep in his recliner. Both of them needed their rest. I dusted off an Adirondack chair on the back deck and pulled my laptop from its bag.

It was a beautiful afternoon, and even with living in town my parents had a quiet neighborhood. The dead-end road they lived on ran into the community playground. The library and historical society buildings were across the street from them. Besides my parents' there were only four other houses on the entire street. When they had bought the house decades before, my dad had chosen this street because it was so quiet. Plus the playground being that close to their home gave my parents free entertainment.

As I logged onto the computer, I had one mission in mind, catching up on life. I had missed so many of the girls' school events that I wanted to get back on track for when I got back home Sunday evening. Kennedy had lacrosse practice two nights and one game the following week. Tryouts were in two weeks for the dance squad, and the extra practices would keep Presley busy until then. Their junior class trip was in three weeks, and we would need to be completely moved out of our house before that.

I emailed a moving company and scheduled an appointment to pack and store most of our belongings. I knew it would only be temporary, but the conversation with Bonnie about the cute Cape Cod came back to me, and I really did begin to feel homeless. "Temporary… just for a while… we will survive this," I said to myself as I paged through old emails. While on the laptop I also scheduled the utilities to be set for transfer into the new owners name and set up a date for our mail to begin to be forwarded to a post office box.

I was engrossed in reading the fine print on the postal service's website when I heard the chair beside me move against the wooden planks. I flinched and turned to see my mom in her robe slide into the seat.

"You doing okay?" I asked.

She nodded, but I could tell there was something more hidden behind her forced smile.

"Are you sure?"

This time she started shaking her head. When she spoke it was just above a whisper. "I'm scared. I woke up and didn't know where I was. Dr. Hamilton warned me about this. I remember that. He told me to wait, that it might come back to me. So I laid there. But it never came back. I started to walk around the house and saw you sitting out here. Then I remembered I was at home. That you were my daughter, Pam, and you were staying with me."

I nodded, watching and waiting for her to continue.

"Seeing you was the only thing that made me remember. It brought me back to today. It just… it feels like I'm lost when I can't remember. To tell you the truth it's like being in a nightmare, yet I can't wake up from it."

My mom needed me. I couldn't leave her. On the other hand, my girls needed me across the state. I was leaving the next morning. I was so torn.

I heard dad join us from the other side. He had a weary smile on his face and opened his mouth to speak. Before he could, I cut him off. "Dad pack a suitcase for you and Mom. You're coming to stay with me and the girls for a while."

The time in the hospital deflated my father. He looked ten years older than when he was visiting us a few weeks before. But when I suggested they come stay with us for a while he looked relieved and stress obviously left his shoulders. He didn't argue, and when Mom started to, he stopped her by telling her it was for the best to listen to me.

I never understood why it was so important for kids to be near aging parents until now. They needed me as much as I needed them.

Chapter Forty-One

The girls were actually happy to see me. They seemed even happier to see their grandparents. I explained that Grandma needed us, and the trips between both sides of the state couldn't go on. Saying they understood, they told me about their weekend, complaining that Bonnie made them work by cleaning the old apartment above the garage, ironically the place we'd be staying. I was glad she didn't tell them my decision, but I knew now I couldn't prolong the inevitable.

"Well, I'm sorry you didn't have a good weekend. Hope you didn't miss anything fun having to work like that," I said with a subtle hint of sarcasm.

If they heard it in my voice, they didn't react. Presley just shrugged while Kennedy shook her head.

"Well then, there's no need to wait any longer. Girls, can I see you out on the back patio?" I ushered them outside before either could complain, shutting the door quietly behind us. I could see Dad pull a chair out for Mom and knew she would have a few demands to keep him busy.

I turned and began talking before they could ask what this was about. "Girls, I wanted to let you know we won't be buying that little house we love."

"Ah, why? We didn't even get to look at it?" Kennedy was obviously disappointed.

"No, we didn't. I'm sorry, but it actually just sold. Probably a blessing actually." I shook my head.

"That's fine. It was probably too small for all your stuff anyway." Presley jabbed her sister in the arm.

She rubbed the sore spot before Kennedy shot back. "Yeah right!

Me with all the stuff? Even though you cleaned out beforehand, did you see how many boxes your room took for packing?"

"So, where are we going?" Kennedy continued. "Did Bonnie find us another place?"

"Funny you should ask. Do you know that apartment you were forced to clean?"

"You've got to be kidding me!" Presley interrupted.

"No I'm actually not. But it's only temporary."

"Thank God," Presley sighed sarcastically. "I don't think I could stand—"

"Let me continue," I said directly to her, showing my seriousness.

"We will only be there for a few weeks, until the end of school. Then, yes, we are moving. But we are moving to King Lake."

Kennedy stood with her mouth hanging open. Of course it was Presley who spoke first though. "Tell me it's only for the summer… It *is* only for the summer, right?"

I just shook my head in response.

"Mom, we're talking about our senior year. We've worked twelve years to get here." This time it was Kennedy to speak, and she did so through developing tears.

"Yes. And you will be a senior and graduate next year no matter what, or where it's from," I explained.

"It's not fair!" Presley stood with her arms crossed and daggers jetting from her eyes. Their target? Me.

My shield went up. I didn't want to fight with them. I hoped for understanding and an alliance. Seeing that neither would be happening, I immediately became defensive. "No, it's not. It's not fair that my mom, the person who raised me—you're grandma—is sick and needs us. I am exhausted. Between repeatedly traveling across the state, taking care of my own mother, and dealing with the emotions of having to see her go through the pain and torment of not remembering who she or her family is—no, it's not fair! See what's missing here? Compassion. From my own kids. I must have failed at teaching you guys that part of life."

Immediately, I had to leave the patio. I knew my anger was the wrong way to be feeling now, but I felt my face scowl before hot tears formed in the corners of my eyes. I didn't want them to see my raw, heartbreaking emotion.

It was more than anger at their reaction. It was sadness at the situation in general and the helplessness I was feeling when all control seemed gone. I knew they would mistake me leaving the conversation as resentment toward them. I would deal with that later. For now, I needed a dark corner, a soft pillow to scream into, and a box of tissues to go through.

Chapter Forty-Two

I was shocked to see that it was Presley who was the one to enter my bedroom first. Her head hung sheepishly telling me she was sorry. Apologies came hard for her, so it was even more shocking when she actually said the words.

"I'm sorry, Mom." She actually meant it.

I patted the bed beside me, and she sat obediently. I draped my arm around her shoulders and laid my head on her. "It's okay. All of this... it's just tough. On all of us. But we're the Taylor family. We stick together. We love together, and yes, we even fight together. It just upsets me to see that we weren't automatically in *this* together."

"It's a lot to swallow, Mom. And, well, it just sucks. We grew up here. We made friends here. The sports, my dance, and everything are all here. I don't want to start over for the last year of our high school," she said, and as she was talking I pulled away to face her.

"I can't imagine being in your shoes. I've had days and many miles home trying to understand how you guys would feel. I told myself that I was going to make it an adventure; another chapter of our lives. It's the twist you never saw coming when you're reading a book," I explained.

"I don't like to read."

"Well then the movies you watch... where you just didn't see that surprising *yet good* part coming."

She nodded in understanding. By now Kennedy was standing in the doorway, and I motioned her in to join us on the bed. She had heard most of our conversation, but I knew I couldn't let them leave without saying more.

"You know, when I was little my mom got pregnant with a boy, my brother." I started talking and saw that I instantly got their attention.

"Yeah, I know you're surprised. I never told you guys about him. Well, Andrew didn't get to be born or even see our mom and dad. He died inside our mom. I was about six, but I remember feeling so much sadness. I lost my brother, but I couldn't imagine ever losing a son. And she did. As I watched her deal with the grief, it was unbearable at times.

Mom would become depressed and just distance herself for weeks and weeks. One day I heard my dad screaming at her from the other room; not fighting *with* her… but fighting to *keep* her. After that, she was normal, mostly. I didn't realize it then, but as I saw her there in her bed at the hospital, and she once again was… was just gone… I understood why he was yelling that day. And now, I know it's my turn to fight to keep her, to get her back."

Kennedy held puddles of tears in her eyes, and her hand covered her mouth. Presley watched me with interest, but as if afraid to interrupt or because she lacked the words to speak, she just sat there.

I continued. "I honestly didn't plan this. Sometimes there is no plan. We are being led in the direction we are meant to go. At all times. We are on a path to serve, to do for the Lord. Even if He says no, it's His answer we obey."

Presley quickly asked, "What if we change that direction or want to do something different?"

"Either you didn't know it but God changed it for you, or He'll just change it right back. Everybody does everything for a reason.

Listen, girls, I know we don't go to church like we should, and that is completely my fault as a mom, but if there is one thing I want for my children it's to understand what God intends and to know that at any time it's completely okay to just give a decision to Him so He can guide you. I had to do that with Mom and the move, or I'd still be worrying over what needed to be done."

Kennedy looked confused. "He was that quick in answering?"

"This time, yes. I prayed for a sign and then woke up the next morning with Bonnie telling me how the house we wanted, the one that was forgotten on the market, suddenly had a contract on it. There's no other explanation. The Lord gave me the sign that quickly. But sometimes it takes a little longer. You may even think

He's not listening. But He is. He's just waiting. You ask for His help, so it's only fair that you wait for Him too."

"Patience hasn't really been my thing," Presley said. Kennedy laughed spilling her tears down her cheeks. She wiped her face and smiled.

I pulled both girls toward me into a hug before continuing, "Maybe that's what you guys need to talk with Him about."

"Maybe," Kennedy croaked the tear-laden words.

Presley got up to leave. "I love you, Mom"

"I love you more," Kennedy stood by her sister and added the comment from a game they played since the girls were both little.

"I love you both the most," I finished the game.

Kennedy closed the door behind her. As they left I added, "Oh, and tell Him I said *hello*."

"Who"? I heard Presley ask.

"The Man upstairs."

Chapter Forty-Three

The next few weeks flew by. When they first arrived I moved Mom and Dad into my bedroom for their stay with us. I knew they would be most comfortable there and the least disturbed while the final touches on the move took place. The day we told the girls our goodbyes for their junior trip to New York we packed my car for a trip for me to take my parents back to King Lake.

Mom made her follow-up appointments for that week. We wanted to get their mail and check on the house too. I began to realize that the best decisions I was making at that moment were through pure faith in God. I knew deciding to move back would be hard.

When I closed the door to our home for the last time I felt joy knowing that He was the one leading me now. I was surprised, but I really didn't feel sadness. The good times we had in the house were still memories in our minds. We weren't leaving them behind.

The only part that I would miss was the growing wall. It's the place in the hallway where the girls would stand to measure their growth each year. I wished I could have packed that piece of the wall, but instead the girls stood on either side of the vertical hash marks as I took their picture. I knew their growing was done now anyway, so it was nothing more than a chapter closed for me.

Another reason for my happiness was that Mom was going to get an updated report from Dr. Hamilton. I was anxious to see what he said. Even though he had encouraged us to not to get our hopes up, it was nice to know that I didn't have to rush home right away and that I could be there for my parents regardless of the outcome.

On the trip back to King Lake, Mom slept most of the way, and Dad refused to let me drive. He said my driving scared him. I knew he just wanted to be in control. He was also the type to turn the radio off and just use the hum of the tires on the road as company. I knew conversation with him probably wouldn't amount to much, so I pulled out a novel I had attempted to read and settled in for a long ride.

I couldn't get involved in the story line though. Just as the words turned into images in my mind and I began to create the plot, I would stop and stare out the window. My mind kept drifting off to the upcoming appointment with Dr. Hamilton. I was curious what he would say, to understand the further testing or procedures Mom might need to endure.

But I was thinking about something more as well. I found myself getting butterflies around the doctor. Not the scared-he-might-give-bad-news kind but rather the I-wonder-how-he-kisses type.

I know it had been a long time since a man had been in my life. Too long. My kids reminded me of it quite often. Now, I was glad I didn't have a significant other to worry about when we moved. It was hard enough taking the kids from their school. I don't know if a guy could be that supportive with this spontaneous decision.

I sighed deeply and looked at the two gray heads in front of me. They made it work. Why was I always making excuses? I may not have had a spouse to uproot with the move, but I also didn't have one for the support needed during this rush of stress I faced. I began to doubt if I'd be okay with the decision now that it was being made.

Chapter Forty-Four

After three days of doctor appointments, confusing diagnoses, and limited options on what to do next, I was exhausted. I fell into the oversized living room chair. There was a soft puff of air from the cushion as I dropped into it, and I couldn't help but feel the same way—deflated. I shut my eyes, but it was only a minute before I heard my mom in the kitchen. She was rattling pans from the cabinet. I looked to my left and could see her stand upright and look at the stove. Then, her eyes shot quickly to the right and back to the stove. She repeated this motion two more times before backing up to the counter and leaning against the hard surface.

I pulled myself from the chair and walked into the kitchen. As I got closer I could see that a look of terror overcast her eyes. When she saw me, she jerked and stared at my face. I immediately did what the nurses suggested that I try.

"Mom, it's Pam. Mom. What's wrong?" I reached for her hand and spoke softly.

Stroking her arm had calmed her while in the many waiting rooms this week. As if she recalled that act of gentleness, the fear left her eyes and tears immediately took their place.

"I just don't remember. I… I start to make something to eat and then I either forget what I wanted to do or I can't find what I need to use. I'm frustrated. I'm sad. But the worst is how scared I am," she said in return.

I couldn't imagine what she was going through, but my motherly instincts took over, and I cradled her in my arms. It was as if she reverted back to a child. She became… me… at eight years old. I was the same way when I realized that even though my friends were practically professionals, skating didn't come as easy to me; when my best friend whizzed through her division test my eyes welled with tears as I panicked on the first question. I was her support now as she was when I was in that situation in the past. She had held me and her arms, and that was the only comfort I needed. I hoped I did the same for her.

Our embrace was interrupted by the phone ringing. From caller ID I could tell it was Dr. Hamilton's office. Expecting a nurse following up on the appointment, when I answered I was surprised to hear Dr. Hamilton's voice on the other end of the line.

"Pam?" he asked, surprised as well that I was the one to answer.

"Dr. Hamilton, I'm so happy to hear from you!" Did I just sound as desperate on the phone as I did in my own head?

"Oh? Is something wrong with your mom since she was here yesterday?" Concern enveloped his voice.

"No... no, no I'm sorry. I was just... Never mind." I turned from the kitchen and walked into the living room again before continuing. "She's okay. She just had a moment in the kitchen. She used to love to cook. Now she doesn't even recognize the place let alone remember the recipes she's made for years."

I heard him draw in a breath as if to gather his thoughts before replying. "I wish the diagnosis had been better, or the future clearer. I have seen patients recover. I have. It just took time. And we can hope for the same for your mom. Listen I called to invite you some place..."

My ears immediately perked up. He couldn't be asking me on a date. Oh no. My face reddened, and I quickly realized my embarrassment was pointless. Then I focused back on his voice.

"This is going to sound odd... even ridiculous maybe..."

And, now I was lost. That's a weird way to ask someone out.

"Every Thursday evening there is a grief meeting held in the fellowship hall at Grace Church. I go, well, at least *try to go* every week."

Before I could ask why I needed to go to a grief meeting, he answered my unspoken question.

"Grief over the loss of a loved one can be similar to bad news, a horrific diagnosis, or just general sadness over a situation. Like that of Mrs. Taylor... I mean your mom." He quickly apologized before continuing, "Anyway, I thought maybe you or your dad might want to try coming to meeting if you want to. Sometimes listening to the stories and encouragement of others makes it just a little better. A little easier."

"But why do *you* go?" I asked, realizing quickly that I shouldn't have done that.

"How about meeting me at the diner tomorrow evening on 5th street at 5:30, and we can get something to eat before the meeting. I'll tell you why I go over the best patty melts this side of the Mississippi."

"I'll be there. Oh, and thank you Dr. Hamilton."

"Please. Call me Travis."

Chapter Forty-Five

Travis? He didn't really look like a Travis. A Ken or a Steve maybe, but not Travis. And then, I realized that I was meeting him for dinner. Alone. Like a date. Well, he probably would think of it as just a meal, in the evening, with another person. I haven't been alone at a dinner table with a man in years. It was as close to a date as I'd been on in a long time.

I turned the television on to a movie marathon of romantic comedies, my mom's favorite. I invited her into the living room and then asked if it was okay if I made dinner that night. I lied and said there was a special meal I've been meaning to make them. She agreed and looked relieved as she sat on the couch diagonally from where I sat. I knew I should have elaborated on what Dr.—I mean, Travis—had mentioned on the phone, that she had to have heard my side of the conversation; but she didn't ask, and I simply stood and headed toward the kitchen.

In the refrigerator Mom had been thawing chicken breasts. I assumed that was what she was going to use for dinner. I also saw a head of broccoli and shredded cheese. I instantly knew she was going to make a broccoli, chicken, and rice casserole; my favorite comfort food from childhood. Instead of inventing something new as I told her, I set out making one of her most common meals. My touch would be garlic herb drop biscuits. The girls taught me how to make them from their Home Economics class earlier that year.

Less than an hour later, I was the last one to pull my chair up to the table. I realized immediately the mood was lighter. My mom smiled and closed her eyes breathing in the smell, maybe triggering a memory of the famous dish of hers. She immediately dug in.

On my other side, Dad was talking incessantly. He was telling how the neighbor's lawnmower caught fire and how he helped put it out with his hose while he was out watering the garden. Then the fire chief, who lives down the street, came to investigate because we were under a strict burn restriction. He thought the neighbor was burning leaves. Every few comments he would take a bite and chew quickly before continuing. We laughed together, Mom included, although I found myself wondering if she remembered she even had neighbors.

I shamed myself. Of course she did. She only had moments. She wasn't *that* far gone.

When he was done and silence fell again I brought up Travis. I told them that he suggested a meeting for me to go to the following night. I had my elbows rested on the table and my glass of water gripped in both hands.

"Why would he invite you and not me?" Mom asked. "Is there something he's keeping from me?"

"No. Not at all." I immediately answered and then regretted bringing it up. I knew there was only one way to appease her. "I actually think it's more of a date."

"Wait! What?!" Dad looked up from the remains of his casserole. "The fine doctor wants to take out my daughter?"

"Yes, apparently, your *grown* daughter will be spending some time with a familiar person of the opposite sex tomorrow," I detailed.

"Wow! Well good for you," he said giggling.

What was wrong with him today? And what did he do with my real dad?

Chapter Forty-Six

I was up with the sun. I was tired, but I couldn't keep my eyes closed. The brighter the room grew, the more anxious I got, and my legs wanted to hit the floor running. I peeked into my parents' room on the way to make coffee. Twenty minutes later I was on my knees weeding the flower beds. Realizing the lack of care they had, I knew my mother's strict attention to making the flowers look prize-worthy may never hold the same love as they had over the years. I would probably be the one in the gardens, and I actually didn't mind the thought of it. The birds singing behind me from the great oak tree made me smile, and before I knew it I was humming an upbeat tune as I worked.

I jerked in surprise when I heard my dad's voice from the patio. "Pam? Everything okay?"

I laughed and sat back on my feet. "Yeah. I just wanted to get out and enjoy the day a little. It's a beautiful morning."

He nodded and then helped me to my feet. "I wanted to tell you that I'm so happy you are here. I just… well… I just feel relieved, I guess."

I wiped my forehead with my right forearm brushing the hair from my eyes before answering him. "That's why you've been in such a good mood, isn't it?"

"I guess that's what you can call it. It's hard to be in a good mood with everything going on. But with you here it's easier. Having the family together…"

"… Minus the girls," I interrupted.

He laughed. "Of course. When will they be home? Sunday?"

"Actually, their flight arrives Saturday evening, so we will have to head back Friday sometime." I stood and wiped my hands on my legs.

He searched for words and then quietly replied, "About that. Maybe we can just stay here. I mean where you're going to stay isn't bigger than a shoebox. I just don't think we need to impose."

"Lucky for you the decision has already been made, and you are both coming. With help from the girls, Bonnie's already set up the guest room in the apartment for you and Mom, and there is an office area that I've put the two twin beds for the girls. I've already claimed the couch so you can't fight me for that. It will be cozy. And I think Mom'll enjoy having the girls near her."

"Sounds more like crowded," he said quietly.

"Just temporary. Remember it's only a few weeks before the girls are out of school. Then, we're coming back here to King Lake. You will have your bed back. And Dr. Hamilton is just a call away if we need him."

He smiled at the mention of the good doctor but still didn't look convinced.

"I know you're worried about her. I am too. We all are. Wouldn't it be easier to have a lot of hands to help than just yours? And the alternative to that is to find a assistance home for her…"

"No way!" he interjected.

"See my point."

"I do. And I know it will be fine. Just hard for me to be dependent. I'm the one that never asks for help. But with her, I just don't know what to do."

"Dad, nobody does. But we can't let her know that."

He reached out and pulled me close in a hug. I whispered my love to him, and he said the same. It was an odd moment as emotion was hard for him to show, and saying the expressions were even harder for him. It made me hold him a little longer, and the way he held back I knew he needed the reassurance.

Chapter Forty-Seven

I left the house at ten after five that evening. I only had to walk a block and a half to get to the diner, but I was anxious to get there. As I crossed the street my parents lived on, I noticed the library looked overgrown with weeds and worse, aged. I wondered the affect, in this day of electronics, how modernization could have an impact on the good old-fashioned bricks and mortar place to actually find a book to read. The parking lot was empty even though the sign read they would be open until six. The building itself was in good shape and large enough to hold thousands of books.

I found myself heading down the sidewalk to the wooden porch and opening the front door. I was greeted by a breeze of air conditioning and dim light. I thought I was alone until I heard coughing from a back room. I wandered around the racks and headed toward where the sound had come from.

"Why hello there. Can I help you young lady?" A small older lady appeared from a small room. She was carrying a small box.

Young lady? I smiled wondering when almost forty became the new young and noted the *Employees Only* sign on the door.

Before I could answer, I recognized the soft blue eyes I was looking into. Her hair may have been bright white and thin now, but the woman in front of me was Mrs. Grayson, the old school librarian from my elementary school. I thought she was ready to retire after my class moved to junior high, but twenty-eight years later, here she was, still working and in a library no less.

"Mrs. Grayson. Oh my goodness. It is so great to see you," I exclaimed, closing the distance between us.

"I'm sorry. I don't remember you, child," she apologized.

"Of course not. I was a student of yours from King Lake Elementary. Pamela Taylor."

Her eyes widened. "Yes, Yes, Pam… I do know you. I remember your curls, and you always helped me with putting books away, but your mom and dad, they live across the street still, don't they." She pointed toward their house.

"Yes. They do." I was impressed with her memory. I didn't want to go into details about what was going on with Mom and knew I had already wasted enough time before meeting Travis. "I am just visiting. I thought I'd check out the library again. But I am in a hurry to meet someone…"

"Oh, well dear. You stop in anytime. This library is as much yours as it is mine, and please tell your parents I said hello." She touched my arm with her cold bony fingers. They shook slightly, and her grip was frail, and her touch was light. In fact it didn't even feel like she touched me at all. Poor woman.

I wanted to hug her, to take in the stale, mothball smell of her sweater, and teleport back to a more innocent time of my childhood. Instead, I thought about her odd comment about her library is mine but dismissed it and replied, "I will Mrs. Grayson. Take care until then."

"Oh, I will, and I'm not worried. You will be back here soon," she said as she turned toward a cart of books.

It was another odd thing to say. I watched her for a second more, shook my head, and headed back outside.

Chapter Forty-Eight

I was nine minutes early when I arrived at the diner. There was a wooden park-style bench in front, and I sat there to wait. My heart began to pound, and I realized I was truly nervous.

"This is not a date," I repeated over and over under my breath. I closed my eyes and took a deep breath. After I released the air from my lungs, I could tell the nerves were still there, and my legs began to bounce. Soon my palms grew clammy, and I flattened my hands hard against my thighs. I did that to both calm my legs as well as dry my hands. I began to chant again that this wasn't a date, and my eyes flew open when I felt someone sit down beside me.

"But I really hoped it was a date." Travis smiled cockeyed at me.

My face grew red, and my eyes became saucers. *Oh My God. That did not just happen.*

"I'm joking!" he said, but it was more of a question.

I did the only thing I could. I jumped to my feet and began to ramble an explanation. "I'm so sorry. No—embarrassed. Then sorry. But it's just been, well so long since I've been anywhere, with anyone, guy-wise, in a long, long time..." By now my hands had made their way to my cheeks, trying to cover the shame that was radiating from them.

"Let's bet. Mine was longer than yours," he said trying to ease my embarrassment.

A couple was leaving the diner, and I took their holding the door as an escape to get inside, to collect my thoughts. A hostess was waiting for us and excitedly showed us to a booth in the back corner. I didn't know if the seclusion would be a good thing or a bad thing. I thanked her and sat down. Travis followed and dropped into the seat across from me.

"So… are you willing to bet?" he asked, not allowing me to remain silent.

I nodded before finding my voice. "Okay. What's the prize?"

He rubbed his chin for a few seconds and then tapped his lips twice. "Dessert. Winner buys dessert."

"Wait, doesn't the loser usually buy?"

"Yeah, but their desserts are winners either way."

I smiled and began to calm down. I looked at the menu for a few minutes before speaking. "Mine is three years."

"Well, go ahead and pick your sweet confection while you're lookin'—seven years this fall," he replied.

"Seven years? Really? That seems impossible."

He gave a hearty laugh. It was genuine. And when he laughed, small lines framed his eyes. I couldn't help but watch all the features as he then talked.

"Yes. It may seem impossible, but it took a long time for me to even want to date, and work kept me from having time to date, and well, before I knew it seven years past. So, if you don't mind, I'd like to call this a date, at least a semi-date?"

I could feel myself begin to blush again, but I nodded. "Okay, fair enough. Semi-date it is. Now you can start your clock over again."

We grew silent long enough to look over the menus. We ordered, then I asked about the meeting that would follow. "So tell me about this grief meeting we are going to."

He chewed his top lip and squinted at me, taking a moment to gather his thoughts. Then he began his story, jumping right in with the details. "My wife… we were married for 2 years… and brother were killed nine years ago."

My jaw dropped. "Both of them? Same year? How tragic."

He shook his head after realizing I didn't quite understand or possibly in preparation to explain. "They were killed while they were together, in a hotel room. It was a drug deal gone wrong. The killer, well dealer, had the wrong room. I was doing my residency at the hospital and spent most nights there. I never knew she was seeing him. They were in the wrong place. They were the wrong people. I should have been there. But regardless I lost two people

I loved. I was mad. I was sad. I was depressed. I couldn't forgive them. I couldn't forgive myself. This group helped me out. So now, I help them out… while they still help me of course." He forced a smile and let me absorb what he just said.

"I am so sorry," I said, forcing myself to find my voice.

"It's okay… now. I just wanted to explain why I go there and why I am here now."

I found myself reach across the table and grab his hand in comfort.

Instead of pulling back he covered my hand with his other one.

Chapter Forty-Nine

I didn't know whether I should jerk my hand away or not. While I tried to decide what to do, our hands stayed entwined on the slick table surface. The server greeted us, apologizing for getting to our table late, and blaming a fired cook for being so backed up on orders. Her presence made us move our hands simultaneously, and mine found their way to my lap. I instinctively rubbed the tingling sensation they mysteriously developed by touching his.

"Ice water with lemon!" I burst out before she could finish asking us what we would like to drink.

"Sweet tea," Travis quickly followed in response.

Was he as nervous as I was? I tried to read his expression but couldn't know for sure.

As I was playing detective he answered my unasked question. "Being here… with you. I'm a little nervous. A semi-date is close enough to a real date and certainly more than anything close to a date that I've experienced in a long time."

"Well, if it makes you feel better I'm just as nervous too. In fact I think I'm going to liven the mood." I slid out of the booth and walked toward the front of the diner. There was a jukebox on the wall. It was a modern digital version, much different from the old one with push buttons that had once sat on the floor below it. I paged through a few selections and typed in two choices. Both upbeat reminiscent songs from our youth. By the time I got back to the booth the first one was playing, and Travis was smiling at the choice.

"My girls won't let me listen to '80s music at home. They say I'm old and so is my taste in music."

"Well, we *are* from the age of male rock stars with big hair, wearing more makeup then our moms who now have gained fifty pounds and are balding," he said in their defense.

"True. Too bad we're just as we were all those years ago."

"Ha, don't I wish," and with that he patted his stomach as if he had gained the weight he talked about. "Hospital cafeterias are not always friendly to those trying to stay young and fit."

"I'm sure neither are difficult patients friendly, and worse are their overbearing families," I added.

The server interrupted us to take our orders. As she left, Travis opened his mouth to speak but took a moment to choose his next words. "You know patients can be difficult, especially when their conditions are so difficult to handle or understand. As a doctor, I've studied, I have learned, and with families you can teach, and they can research to learn more, but with a patient they may never understand."

"That's why you want me, well, people *like* me, to find a support group?" I asked.

"Yes. That's exactly right. The families who learn more, who understand and have done their homework, make it easier to build the bridge for the patient to understand as well… or, if nothing more, to become comfortable maybe not with their diagnosis but just around those near them, their support system."

I played with my straw in my ice water, making the ice clink against the sides and then I told him my plans to take Mom to the coast for a few weeks, until school ended and then relocate with my girls back here to King Lake.

His eyes seemed to brighten. I hoped it was to spend more time with me. Then he spoke. "Wow! That is wonderful for your mom. She will be so much better when you are a constant near her. When you went home, she would change, draw inside herself like a turtle retreating into its shell. I know, bad analogy. But it would honestly be days before she would get a light back again. I haven't seen that light dim like that since you've been here."

"Really? I haven't seen any of that."

"No, you wouldn't. As an outsider looking in, I do. I see it with families because I'm around it so often. Trust me. It's there."

And I instantly did trust him. I had before or course, as my mom's doctor, but this was different. I trusted him as a friend.

Chapter Fifty

The meal was delicious, but the company was better. Travis was right with saying the diner's patty melts were the best I would ever have, but being able to spend time with someone who could make me laugh and who understood my situation; that was priceless.

The meeting would start at 7:00. We walked the short distance down the street side-by-side in silence. We let our conversation and dinners digest in the peace of the evening.

We were a few minutes early when we arrived at the church. There were a few people milling around. I didn't recognize any of them. But it had been years, literally a lifetime ago, since I would have seen them, and I expected them to not know me either. Travis set to saying hello to everyone. You could tell his presence offered much needed comfort, and everyone enjoyed the moment he arrived. I was awestruck as the people began to close around to welcome him, as if he was the special guest or a celebrity in town on tour. As I began to pull away, allowing him space, he held onto my upper arm, pulling me closer.

It caught me off guard, but before I could argue he introduced me around to everyone. "This is Pam Taylor. You may remember her from growing up years ago in this area, but you surely know her parents who are still here…" he began.

"Ah yes, how is your dear mom doing?" an older gentleman, who I came to learn was named Bob Dooley, interrupted with a raspy voice.

A woman to my left touched my hand with her cold fingers. "We heard she was ill, is that right?"

I tried to speak, to address the two of them before someone else piped in, but I wasn't quite sure I knew what to say or whether I even wanted to say anything.

"She's better every day, and it's Pam's first time here, so we should keep the questions for later." Travis spoke for me and ushered me through the crowd making it to the church entrance in seconds.

I shook my head, and Travis offered a friendly shove into the meeting room. Blinking, I took in the well-lit, open room. It had a musty smell, as most church fellowship halls did. There were people talking, some standing around. Others sat in silence. Nobody looked up as I shuffled quickly to a seat in an empty row near the back.

I took the time to sigh softly to myself wondering how the next hour would play out, and wondered if all my adrenaline and mental energy was spent walking through the door.

Chapter Fifty-One

Her name was Ronny. Actually it was Veronica Pearson…well, now it's Hughes. I should have remembered her from school since she was just a few years younger with me, but the older I get the faster I forget my younger years; faster even than I could make new memories.

I sat in complete silence as she spoke from the front right of the room. She told of the tragedy that happened to her just eight months ago. This was her first meeting, the first time that was able to speak in public about her life. While she was with her mom and two young children shopping for back to school clothes, her dad and husband attended an out of town baseball game. It was late when they were driving home. After leaving the stadium, just two miles down the interstate they encountered a drunk driver going the wrong way. They swerved to avoid a head-on collision and careened down a steep embankment rolling until they came to rest on their roof. Paramedics pronounced her husband dead on the scene, and her father was left a paraplegic. She spoke calmly, and while doing so the room remained quiet.

When she finished, she lowered her teary eyes and thanked everyone for allowing her to be there to tell her story and to feel welcome among the group. Travis, who sat at the front, now stood and walked to Ronny's side hugging her lightly before the woman sat down. He was the unofficial leader of the meeting, but you could see his compassion for someone who had also been in a similar position.

I felt so much sympathy for her but at the same time out of place, as her story, like Travis' was so tragic compared to my situation. My mom was alive. They lost family. Looking around I could see pain in other people's faces as well. I knew they were probably holding similar stories; that was until the next person spoke.

Zack Sealy, a twenty-four-year-old father of two boys, found out that his youngest, just eighteen months old, had leukemia. As he prepared for the worst the doctors slowly gave him pieces of hope. He said it was worse than a roller coaster in the dark. Not only did the track go up and down on the ride, you couldn't see what was coming next. I instantly related to him. He wanted to be happy for the small positives but knew that if he did he might be blindsided in the end. I sat there simply nodding.

An older gentleman stood before Zack sat down and told the story of his sister, also suffering from cancer. But in his case she was now on hospice, and they were making final arrangements. He agreed with Zack's cautious attitude, because he and their family were given a positive outlook after she made it to remission twice. An error in a brain scan misdiagnosed the size of the tumor, and now, here they were.

Others spoke with new or similar situations—each one given full attention by the audience, some heads nodding, others with eyes downcast afraid to show their true expressions. The hope and patience to heal was explained by allowing time and distractions to intervene.

Having seen all angles of grief, I understood why Travis wanted me here. I caught his eye as he looked back at me and smiled. As if he knew what I was thinking, he winked.

That is when the butterflies first took flight in my stomach.

Chapter Fifty-Two

The *semi-date* was a few days past but still fresh on my mind. We were back at Wellington Beach now, crammed together in Bonnie's apartment. The girls had arrived back safely that afternoon from New York. They talked nonstop about the sites seen during their visit—Kennedy about real geographical sites, Presley about the boys.

Other than the cramped space and Mom and Dad as additional permanent guests, life as I knew it was normal again. I leaned back on the couch and pulled my legs in close while sipping a glass of wine. I was never much of a drinker, but a good glass of wine was always welcome. This one was bought by Bonnie as a pseudo housewarming gift. The name of the wine was *Change is Good*. Fitting. Knowing Bonnie, that was the reason she bought it. But it was also very flavorful. Sweet, deep red, and fruity. Perfect.

As I sat in silence, enjoying my gift, I thought of those last moments spent with Travis, and those same giddy teenage feelings came back again. I surprised myself with having so much in common with Presley. She couldn't contain her excitement about boys that she met and the numbers she exchanged… looking for the perfect opportunity to get to use them… and I couldn't wait to find a reason to spend more time getting to know the friendly doctor.

As I sipped from my glass letting the warmth of the alcohol travel to the tips of my fingers, two thoughts fought for space at the front of my mind. One—I really was not a drinker, and now I know why. And two—I remembered dragon boy and the day at the jail that wasn't so-long-ago. I'll stick with grown-up relationships. Presley can have her crazy ones.

Chapter Fifty-Three

Sitting on one of the small stools at a makeshift breakfast bar that Thursday morning, I watched as the girls got ready for school. They weren't accustomed to riding the bus. Against their will, they gave up the car to their grandparents. I wanted to make sure they had a vehicle in case of an emergency, and the bus still drove by the house twice a day. So there was no reason they couldn't give up their car and use the free transportation for a few weeks.

I did feel bad since they had just gotten it for their birthday and then couldn't even drive it for the last few weeks of school. After some light bribery involving weekend use of my car with a full tank they both agreed.

Presley was usually the slow one, but today she was standing by the door rolling her eyes and sighing deeply while waiting for her sister to join her for the short walk to the bus stop. With each sigh she took a sip of water from a disposable bottle. Her breakfast I assumed.

"I *am* hurrying. I'm just so tired. I couldn't sleep on that hard mattress. I would have gone to the couch, but it was in use." Kennedy rushed around as she gathered her books for school.

"I know. You almost sat on me," I said.

"Looks like I'm gonna be late—and I *can't* be late."

Presley gasped. "What? Perfect Kennedy is going to be late? When does the parade and fireworks begin for this festive occasion?"

"Being late is being selfish, Kennedy... and that goes for you too Pres."

"Nobody will be there waiting," continued Kennedy.

I shook my head not understanding. "Then if there is no time requirement, why are you worried about being late."

"Because I'm *always* the first one there."

"Gag. Me," Presley exaggerated.

"Kennedy, I think it's time I taught you about priorities and stress and something called Obsessive Compulsive Disorder for that matter," I interjected.

At that moment Presley literally did gag, well choke, on her water.

"Well, you did ask for it," Kennedy said through clenched teeth.

Chapter Fifty-Four

Even though my work was still very part-time, I dove into anything I could find to do every day that I was in the office. As much as I hoped the time would go by quickly, I did enjoy my time in the office. I needed the time away from the close confines of my home to catch my breath.

I was happy the girls had school. They had each day to be the teenagers they needed to be and could use the distraction from the crowded apartment as well. Mom and Dad were content to take care of the dogs. They didn't want to be fussed or hovered over, just like we didn't want to do that to them. So I kept my distance, even if it meant walking around the park or reading at the library.

After speaking with Mrs. Grayson in King Lake, I realized the enjoyment I once had spending time in the library as a child. As I watched people come and go throughout the day while I was there for hours, it gave me hope that people do still use the old brick and mortar version of what can be found conveniently through electronic devices.

But today I wasn't spending quiet time people watching and browsing the fiction shelves at the library. It was a work day at the Realtor's office. I was filtering email requests from the website and responding to the easy ones with generic answers of, "Thank you for contacting us, here is the information you requested…"

Between sending pictures of new listings, public tax records of land parcels, and contact information for the agents I was ready to finally see five o'clock come. That afternoon I was picking up the girls at separate friends' houses and pizza in between both places. I wish they could share friends the way they used to share a bed. Unfortunately they were twice as different, which made me twice as tired.

Chapter Fifty-Five

I was sitting in the driveway at Kennedy's friend Sarah's house. She was finishing up with a history project and asked that I give her a few minutes. Beside me Presley played a game on her phone while balancing the hot pizzas on her lap.

"I'll put them in the back if you want me to." I nodded toward the boxes.

"Nah—they're okay," she said without looking up.

"Okay. Well, how was school then?"

"Same."

"Same as what?" I was losing patience.

"Just same."

I grabbed her phone in one swift motion.

She threw a look of horror in my direction. "Why… what…"

Before she could formulate thoughts and express them to me I cut her off. "You will look at me when I'm talking to you. You will respect me enough to answer with more than one syllable, one word answers. *And* you will check your attitude at school before we see each other. Do you understand?"

Her wall of emotion visibly crumbled. "No. I don't understand. I don't understand how you can just make us move. And *you* don't understand how Kennedy and I feel about any of the changes—moving, grandma and grandpa staying with us, moving *again*. And finally leaving school and friends we've been with for twelve years!" Her voice grew increasingly louder the longer she talked.

It didn't take me long to prepare my answer. I knew what I was going to say, but Kennedy was walking toward the car by now and since her sister threw her name into the steaming pot of issues she had with me I figured I might as well save my breath and address both of them at the same time.

"What's with all the serious faces?" she asked falling into the backseat with her arms overflowing with textbooks and folders.

I brought Kennedy up to speed on the subject at hand, and then I answered them both.

"No, you're right. I don't understand. How could I. I am not in your shoes. And I would never expect you to understand my situation or feelings either. But I'm tired of people holding in their feelings until they explode in a fit of rage. You are no longer toddlers, so don't act like one! You have a voice, and you are required as a lady to use it. I even encourage it… when used correctly that is.

"When I moved away from my home, my family, I didn't know how to ever begin to start over in a new place. I won't lie to you. You're going to be lonely. You're going to miss this area, our old home. But at least you have each other."

With that, I handed Presley her phone back and backed out of the driveway. I looked in the rear view mirror at Kennedy who was simply looking at her hands in her lap.

Chapter Fifty-Six

When we got back to the apartment, I threw the pizza boxes on the counter, ignored my father's protests and questioning, and headed to the bathroom. I shut the door and locked it, sliding down the wood and sinking onto the tile. The apartment was so small this was the only place to find peace.

I didn't waste my moments alone feeling sorry for myself or questioning my decision to move, instead I tried to rewind back to when I was their age, to understand what was going on in their world at that moment. Although times have changed and life was different, a teenager will always be a teenager. I wouldn't blame them for acting out. We all did at that age.

After twenty minutes I had a plan. I needed to be on their level now, to be in their shoes.

"Girls, can you come here for a minute."

I stood by the bathroom door and waited for them to come. By then their plates with half-eaten crusts were being thrown away as they walked silently in my direction.

I ushered them into the lone bedroom and shut the door behind me. I didn't hesitate before beginning to speak.

"I understand what you are going through. You must remember, at one time I had to move too. I had to make a new life. I only ask you to give me one year of your life. I don't care where you go to college. You can come back here. You can keep in touch with your friends, and we can even come back and visit. I would give you my life if I had to. I'm only asking for one year. And I understand you are both into activities that they may or may not have at our new home. They have activities in the next school district we don't have here. Every school is different, but you *will* find something else to do."

"But I dance, Mom. That is what I *do*. You can't expect me to play volleyball or join the choir. I don't *do* that. I *dance*," Presley interrupted.

"I know. I don't expect you to learn something new. You know you were meant to dance. I know you were meant to dance. That is why you do it so well. Maybe you can take classes at a private studio. Or maybe you're meant to give that knowledge to others, and teach afterschool at the studio. "I'm only asking for a year—*one* year. I gave you seventeen while my family was on the other side of the state."

Kennedy spoke up for the first time since the car ride. "I know they won't have lacrosse. *Nobody* has lacrosse, and I was good at it. I thought I'd even get a scholarship one day…"

After she trailed off, I walked toward her and put my hands on either shoulder. "You still can. Scholarships are in every aspect of life. Just because one door closes doesn't mean God won't open another one or two in its place, even if you have to look harder to find it."

Presley rolled her eyes mocking her sister. "Yeah, of course Kennedy doesn't care. Kennedy's always the good child. The one that always wants to make people happy. The one who can't ever argue with Mom, nor have Mom mad at her. It's annoying. Not to mention pathetic. When are you gonna stop competing for the title of Mom's Favorite Daughter?"

Kennedy spoke up. "I can do whatever I want. Say whatever I want, and be however I want. Call me a suck-up or pathetic. I don't care. I hardly think I'm trying to be her favorite. Try more like respectable." She added in a whisper, "Not that you know what that means."

Before Presley could argue, I spoke. "You know, you are twins. *Identical* twins—you are supposed to like and do the same things. Your personalities should be the same. But you couldn't be more different. What is wrong with this picture?"

"Can I go now?" Presley asked as her answer.

I nodded as she walked by me and opened the door. "But don't forget—*one year*."

I didn't have to see her face to know she rolled her eyes again. She may be a difficult child, but one thing was sure; she was predictable.

Chapter Fifty-Seven

It was a week later, and I actually thought about canceling the plans to move. Mom had a good day yesterday. From the time she woke up until I said good night she seemed *better*. Yes, she had been generally quiet, but she didn't act scared, forgetful, or drift off into her now usual childlike behavior. It was a good day.

Today, on the other hand, was not good. All those fantasies of canceling the move quickly disappeared as I now sat comforting her as she cried into my shoulder shaking from distrust after I had to once again show the familiar family picture I now carried around with me. It was the proof she needed that she was in fact my mother. In it my parents and I sat with our arms around each other at our old table, playing a board game.

It was from Thanksgiving two years before. Kennedy took the picture right before she tripped over Lexi and the camera shattered on the hardwood floor. Having salvaged the flash drive from the rubble allowed me to keep the memories of that day alive. Now, the well-used picture was folded, torn on one side and overly handled, resembling the fractured camera from that day.

In the end, the nightmare that we went through that time lasted a little over twenty-four minutes. I know the exact timing because I had just put a load of laundry into the washing machine in Bonnie's garage when the blood curdling scream echoed from the house.

My mother had woken up in an *unknown* bed and was face to face with an *unknown* man beside her. As I had rocked her in my arms after showing her the picture, she allowed me to give her some medicine to calm her, and she laid back down. Dad was now holding his head in his hands. I went to his side of the bed and settled beside him draping my arm across his back and letting my head fall to his shoulder.

The end-of-cycle buzzer sounded on the washing machine. Twenty-four minutes.

"I love you, and I'm here for you as much as I am for her, Dad. You know that don't you?" I whispered.

He swallowed hard and nodded once, never lifting his head.

As I got up and grabbed the next load of laundry, I sighed and consoled him with words even more important that he needed to hear. "I'm calling Dr. Hamilton as soon I get back from downstairs."

Chapter Fifty-Eight

I waited on hold for twelve minutes before Dr. Hamilton got on the line. I had already had an exasperated office worker try to convince me to have him call me back twice before he picked up the extension. Instead of been annoyed himself, he was extremely pleasant as he spoke.

"Good morning, Dr. Hamilton."

I had assumed Lisa, the secretary, had surely let him know who was waiting, but if she did, his casual introduction caught me off guard. "Hello, I mean, Hi, Dr... I mean Travis—its Pamela Taylor."

"Oh, Pam, it's so good to hear from you. I wondered how everything's been going. How's your mom?"

"Actually. That's why I am calling. I didn't want to do this. I wanted to be able to handle everything, hoped it would get better, but this has been the roughest day yet. I don't know what to do." And from there I told him everything that had happened up until that point. How one day was good but the next was not and the emotional ride the family was taking was exhausting.

He listened and calmly expressed his sincere apology for not having a quick or even foreseeable solution. I could tell he held a personal connection, if only because of our dinner together. His sentiment was real. I knew he meant his heartfelt concern for the family and that it wasn't the same *sorry-about-your-dreaded-issues* spiel that most patients heard from a doctor. I could hear him noting everything I was saying, and he asked questions to understand better the solution needed. In the end he decided to change her medication regime.

"Don't get upset or be surprised if she is tired. All the time. Until this new medication gets regulated into her system the best thing for her is to rest. So, when are you coming back this way?" His question sounded two-fold, or maybe I just hoped for more. But before I could read too much into it he clarified what he said. "I mean, I would like to see her as soon as you guys are back."

"Of course. And we would like you to see her too. I think she has questions that her doctor can answer better than us. I'm just sorry we aren't already back there. If circumstances were different we'd already have her home." And then I explained that plans were to leave as soon as the girls were out of school.

Travis quickly closed the conversation, noting his next patient was just taken back to an exam room. "Let's get together when you're in King Lake again—outside the office, okay?"

I felt a wave of chill sweep up my body. It took me a few seconds to make the words come out. "Sounds good," I finally said, and before I could even thank him for helping me with Mom, I pushed the disconnect button on my phone.

Chapter Fifty-Nine

"Don't forget the leashes," I yelled through the open apartment door. Kennedy was helping me with the last bags as we packed the car for the move to King Lake. The sun was barely shining over the horizon, but we were already running behind. The last day of school had been that past Friday, but because Presley had to stay an extra day to pass the proverbial *torch* to the newest group of dance team members Saturday afternoon, we were now leaving Sunday morning.

Since coming back home from the party she hadn't spoken a word to any of us. Instead of helping, especially since we were running behind because of *her* needs, she was now sitting on the curb scrolling through a social app on her phone. She was probably updating her status on how much she hated me, or the family, and most definitely the move.

I walked over to her, crossed my arms and spoke softly. "You have a choice as to which car you ride in. Personally, I'd like the quietness, so I don't mind if you ride with me. But you have twenty seconds to get into one of these vehicles before I load you onto the roof."

She looked up, sighed loudly, and stood although not moving toward either car. I turned away from her and walked into the house for one last look around. She was so ungrateful.

In doing my last minute inspection, my final room was actually the hall closet. It was as big as the bathroom we all shared and had ended up being a lifesaver for storage as this is where the girls kept their clothes for the last few weeks.

There, along the side wall was Presley's laptop, propped behind a shelf that had fallen. I chuckled with deceit as I quickly carried it out to my car and hid it behind the driver's seat. She had her back to me the entire time, still standing between the cars playing on her phone. She finally looked up and saw me smiling at her as I sank into the driver's seat. One word fell off my tongue as I looked back. *Bribery*.

She cocked her head in confusion as she tried to understand what I had just said and walked around and sulked into the seat beside me.

I kept that smile on my face for many miles into the trip.

Chapter Sixty

Looking in the rearview mirror I was surprised to feel the raw emotion I had from leaving. Even though I was born in King Lake, my roots had taken hold at Wellington Beach. The only sand we'd see in our near future would be what moved with us in the car.

I guess I wouldn't miss the salty air that much. Although good to keep the allergies at bay, it was terrible on our hair and the vehicles. I realized the sound of sea gulls would be a missed alarm clock in the mornings. Grandfathered into the city codes, George Nelson, Mom and Dad's neighbor did have a pet rooster that would surely take that place.

I would miss Bonnie. She had done so much for us and for me as a best friend. She was everything I needed, when I needed her most. Not wanting to wake her that morning I left a note expressing my thanks and love for her and that I would call as soon as I got there. The love I felt for her was like that of a sister I didn't have. I hoped she knew that.

It made me wonder why my girls weren't that close. Or were they and I just didn't see it. I looked at Presley in the seat beside me, still slumped over, with her earphones on and thumbs still dancing on the screen of her phone. What I witnessed was constant bickering, disagreeable comments, and personalities as opposite as their wardrobes.

As I had prepared for their birth I spent many hours in the library reading every book they had on their shelves about birthing and raising twins. Every one spoke of how twins, especially those that were identical, would have a bond nobody could sever. Was the bond so hidden that I just couldn't see it? Immediately I was slammed with the thought that I haven't spent time with them to truly understand what was going on with them? I have been so busy with Mom, the move, and, selfishly, me. Before I could stop them, tears pooled quickly and fell rapidly down my face.

I glanced out the driver's window and with my left hand quickly wiped my face. I looked back in Presley's direction hoping she didn't see. But she did. And in her eyes I read shock. And something else, probably pain. I couldn't tell. I just raised the corners of my mouth into a smile, and she silently smirked her own smile back to me and then turned back to her phone in silence.

Chapter Sixty-One

It was a little over four hours into the trip, and both cars were heading towards empty. As I pumped gas Presley leaned against the front of the car with her arms crossed and her ear buds draped around her neck. The music was so loud I heard every word five feet away. Kennedy had made a point to run from the pump the other car was at just to give me a hug. She and my parents were heading inside to grab a bite to eat from the attached hamburger restaurant.

"I do not have cash," I answered Presley's request for money.

"You do too have money," she argued.

"I didn't say I didn't have money. I said I don't have cash. I have plastic. Plastic cannot be shared."

"Molly uses her mom's card all the time. She trusts her with it. And I need to get something in the store."

I finished pumping and headed inside to pay. "I don't care what Molly and her mom do. You're not Molly, and I'm not her mom. Now, if you need me to get something for you while we're in the store, I can get it."

She followed me into the gas station and quickly set to shop for what she needed: a drink from the cooler, two kinds of candy bars, corn chips, a pair of overpriced sunglasses, and box of even more overpriced tampons. She threw it all on the counter as I handed my card to pay for the gas to the cashier. Then, as if remembering at the last minute she grabbed a bag of beef jerky and two packages of bubble gum to add to the pile.

I looked at her with wide eyes. "Are you sure you don't need anything else? I mean there is still stuff on the shelves."

"I told you I needed some things," she replied with a smile, the first one I had seen on her face since we left.

The young cashier looked to me for a reaction. When I didn't bat an eyelash she laughed and started to scan the leaning tower of merchandise.

Chapter Sixty-Two

It was after dinner when we finally made it to Mom and Dad's house. As the girls and I unpacked, I explained that once again they would be sharing a room and also share the dresser and closet space for now. Then I left them to put their stuff away while I opened the laptop and searched for nearby storage units. It felt like part of me didn't make the trip knowing our furniture and most of our belongings were locked in storage in Wellington Beach. I emailed a few units for pricing and was surprised, as late as it was in the day, to actually get a response from a few of them. By 8:00 I had scheduled times to look at them after Mom's doctor appointment the next day.

I was browsing around the internet looking for part-time positions when I heard soft footsteps enter the room. I looked up in time to see Kennedy fall into the soft sofa cushion. She looked how I felt, exhausted. She didn't say a word—just laid her head back—and I went back to opening windows on the internet.

A few minutes went by, and I couldn't help but say aloud, "Well isn't that odd?"

Kennedy opened her eyes and looked in my direction as if too tired to even ask, *What?*

"There is a position open at the library," I continued.

She sat more upright, adjusting the pillows behind her. "Why is that odd?"

"Last time I was here I stopped in there. I had a nice talk with the librarian. Turns out she was an old teacher of mine from elementary school. She didn't mention there was an opening though."

"Are you going to apply? I mean, I never saw you as a librarian. You just aren't... well... *old*... I guess," Kennedy said.

"*Hmmph.* You don't have to be old to be a librarian. Look at Miss Panetta in your elementary school. She was younger than I was when you went there."

"Mom! She was a substitute because Mrs. Garrison retired. She was there until that retched Ms. Wesley came. Ugh. Talk about a mean old lady."

"Okay, okay. Point made, although not well taken."

She sat quietly for a few minutes, then laid her head back. With her eyes closed again she asked, "You're still going to apply though, aren't you?"

"Oh yeah. You can help me pick out the blouse to go with the pearls and my new permed doo for my interview."

She laughed without opening her eyes and added, "Presley will be so embarrassed if you work there."

"Only when I wear that outfit." I laughed too.

I let a few minutes lapse before I asked her the burning question I had on my mind the entire ride across the state. "I know I was being selfish, at least I feel that way, having to move us the whole way over to this side of the state. You had to leave your friends and school and your life. Tell me honestly how you are feeling about everything?"

This time when she opened her eyes she leaned forward and rested her arms on her thighs. "I am scared. I was sad. I was angry. But I'm over all of that. Friends will stay friends, or they weren't meant to be. I broke up with Mike weeks ago, so this is actually a good escape from that drama. I don't know—I'm just scared of the new school year to come. I'm sure this summer I'll make friends here, so it won't be so bad come August."

"Thank you. I needed to hear that. I just wish your sister felt the same."

"I think she does, or at least she will. Eventually," Kennedy reassured me as she stood to let the dancing dogs out that were at her feet.

Chapter Sixty-Three

The clock was pushing toward the ten o'clock hour, and I was finally able to convince my mom to get into the car. She refused to go anywhere with me since she once again had reverted back to not recognizing her family.

When I asked her who she wanted to see instead, she told me Judy, who I remembered was a good friend in high school. Although she had passed away seven years before, I told her we were going to see her. I hated to lie, and I honestly didn't even know if the trick would work. But I was surprised—it did.

We only had minutes to spare before the appointment. Kennedy was on the couch watching a talk show. There was laughing from the audience and what appeared to be a dog jumping in and out of a tall box. She chuckled along with it. Presley had yet to emerge from the bedroom. She was great at a lot of things—unfortunately, holding a grudge topped the list.

From behind the couch I quickly kissed Kennedy's head while simultaneously patting the dogs that were stretched out beside her. Kennedy waved goodbye, too entranced with the screen to look up. I shuffled Mom to the car, where Dad was waiting, and I sank into the back seat sighing as I let my head fall backward. He looked at me in the rearview mirror, and I just shook my head.

As we all rode in silence, I made mental lists of how often she was having her episodes. Surprisingly, they did seem less frequent. Sadly though, they seemed to be more intense and longer when they did occur. I would remember to tell Dr. Hamilton that.

I closed my eyes and smiled. The thought of seeing him relaxed me. I felt awful for looking forward to Mom's appointments to see him. What terrible circumstances to have such desire for a person. I shook my head and briefly closed my eyes.

It wasn't that I was asleep, but nonetheless I was startled upright when my Mom yelled out, "Judy is dead! She's *dead*! How come you told me we are going to see her?"

Good grief. Now what?

Chapter Sixty-Four

Seventeen minutes. That is how long it took to get her into the office. I had called ahead and let the receptionist know about the situation. I think mom was just mad that we tricked her into coming. By the time she signed in at the window, she was back to *normal*. They called her to the room before she even sat down. Dad and I trailed behind in silence. As the nurse shut the door, I could tell Mom wanted to say something.

"I'm sorry," she simply said.

I borrowed the doctor's wheeled stool and pulled myself over to her. Hugging her close, I whispered into her hair, "You have nothing to be sorry about. I wish we could all say what we feel at any moment. You just have the excuse to actually do it."

She laughed. Hard. And before I knew it we were both laughing until tears rolled down our faces. It was like the sluice gates had opened, and we threw all tension into the childish healing that giggling offered. Dad, who hadn't heard anything I said, joined in because I am sure we were a crazy sight to take in.

Dr. Hamilton knocked on the door, and as if we were kids in an elementary classroom we shushed each other.

He gave us all warm smiles but didn't comment on the laughs he must have heard from the hall. He shook each one of our hands, ending on mine and holding it for just a few seconds longer than the other two.

I pulled away, probably more abruptly than I wanted and told him what I had thought of in the car. He was already aware of her outbursts I was sure.

"Actually, I am very glad that you said that." He stopped for a second before continuing, "I mean, I have done extensive research on your case Mrs. Taylor. I have seen how all four examples evolved. This one that you are speaking of has a positive outlook.

"Four examples? What are they?" I asked.

"Well there is of course the case of getting completely better, like this," he snapped his fingers.

We all gave him a discouraging look.

"There is the nothing-happens-and-it-stays-the-same case. Then there is the getting-more-frequent-episodes, and the case like your mom has, fewer episodes."

"But they seem to be—"

"Worse. I know," he finished my sentence and shifted from one foot to another moving mom's chart to his hip. "But in all of those cases, so did the patient. At least that is the initial thought. Think back, closely. Are they worse? Or are you seeing them more clearly and able to document and remember more of the episode because they all didn't run together?"

I looked at Dad. As if I could read his mind we both immediately rewound to the past few days, weeks. As if our idea light bulbs lit together we nodded in unison. He was right.

"Mrs. Taylor," he knelt down and held her tightly clasped hands in her lap, "I'm not promising a miracle. I can't say you will get better. I understand that it's scary. It will be scary, for a long time. And it may never get completely better. But I have a better idea of the path I need to help you on this journey. Do you trust me? Will you allow me to help? Will you allow your husband and daughter to help?"

She looked like a small child, but slowly nodded her head.

Seeing him talk to Mom like that made my heart melt. He was so compassionate. He loved his work. I saw his desire to heal, and I fought the urge to get up and grab them both into an embrace.

As we gathered the latest round of *new and improved* prescriptions for Mom's medicinal regime, Dr. Hamilton held the door and said goodbye. Dad and Mom walked out while I stayed behind. I wanted to thank him for his encouragement. I was surprised when he spoke first. And even more surprised with what he said. "I want to take you out. Tonight. On a real date."

"Tonight? I just got in town. I can't tonight," I replied.

"I am so sorry. I knew that." He chuckled then continued, "Okay, when is better? Maybe Friday—if I can call you?"

I couldn't think of an excuse even if I wanted to. But I didn't want to appear too desperate. So I said what any good romance movie taught me to say.

"Call me."

Chapter Sixty-Five

The new medications did make Mom tired, just as Travis said they would. She slept more than she was awake. The downfall to that was the bursts of sleep gave her insomnia at night. The light of the television shone down the hall into my room each night. It was actually a relief to see it. I knew if she was awake and not confused about who she was, the medicine must be working. After watching the light dance along the doorway for a few minutes, I turned and closed my eyes. I drifted into the deepest sleep I had in weeks.

I was shaken abruptly awake with the slamming of the front door. I grabbed my robe and headed to the front of the house dressing in the process. I took note of the time on kitchen clock as I passed. It was 8:50. I can't believe I slept so late.

Outside, Presley stood on the steps with her arms crossed and her back to me. She was in her pajamas. Kennedy was standing by the car with one foot in as if getting ready to leave. I opened the door, and Presley spun around to face me with fire in her eyes.

"She *can't* take the car, Mom."

I looked around her at Kennedy. "Where are you going?"

Before she could answer Presley unfolded her arms and held them out to her sides. "I need the car today. She *can not* take it."

"Presley, calm down and be quiet. I am talking to your sister right now." I stepped out to the front porch and closed the door behind me. I hadn't heard Mom or Dad and assumed they too might have slept in.

"Kennedy, *where* are you going?" I repeated.

She stepped back out of the car and held up a file, "I have four applications to turn in. I printed these off yesterday when you were at the doctor's office."

"Job hunting, huh?" I asked rhetorically. I turned and looked at Presley. "Now, why do *you* need the car?"

"I just need it," was her reply through clenched teeth.

I tilted my head and crossed my arms. "Sorry, in this competition, you lose with that answer. If you want to put applications in with your sister you can ride along, with her… in the car… together."

She shook her head violently in disagreement. Then realizing it was her only wheels, and those wheels were leaving, she changed her mind and agreed. "Fine. I need twenty minutes to get ready."

I motioned with my head to my other daughter and with slight sarcasm said, "Kennedy, come inside for a minute. Your sister wants to ride along and needs to get ready. She needs to look good for potential interviews."

Chapter Sixty-Six

King Lake is more of a community than a town. The school houses kindergarten through 12th grade, and the closest thing to a restaurant is the grill-slash-diner that I ate at with Travis. Most places can be walked to and most people commute to work in surrounding towns. Because of this the girls applied at the fast food establishments and stores in Lawrence City, which, in itself is not very *city-like*. It's actually more like *big-town*.

Lawrence City is about eight miles to the west of King Lake, and this is where both girls found a job at Pick and Pack, a local grocer to the area. Because they shared a ride their schedules would be the same. This would be an interesting adventure for both of them. Kennedy was, of course, excited to know someone she was working with, while Presley was depressed with the idea of having to work at all.

"You can't stay depressed forever, Pres," I said as I sprayed and wiped the kitchen counter. "You have to face the fact that this is where we will be living, at least for the time being. You can't stay mad at me forever, and you *will* have to create a life here now. It's as simple as that."

"I know I didn't have a choice to move, but I do have a choice whether I'm happy or not," she replied with folded arms.

"True, you can be unhappy, but your life would be a lot easier if you weren't." I stopped cleaning and faced her. "Do you understand that you moving here isn't the end of the world and that some of us," I pointed to myself, "not only had to quit my life in that place to move but also have to deal with a sick mother and depressed father as well? If I were you, I'd take my sulking self to my room to think about how selfish I've been acting."

I turned and began cleaning again, more agressively this time. Presley stared at me a few seconds before she left. I didn't know if I should cry or scream. What could possibly make that girl understand and be less angry with her own self and with life in general? I steadied my shaking hand to finish wiping and then sank down onto the bar stool and dropped my head into my hands.

I wasn't a drinker, not even socially. That was apparent with Bonnie's gift of wine. But that girl right there was going to cause me to start.

Chapter Sixty-Seven

By Wednesday afternoon I had to get out of the house. The weather was absolutely gorgeous, and even though I had a ton of work around the house to help Mom and Dad out, I was ready to visit my old hometown some more. The main street was set up as seen in the old western days. The slanted parking spots were rarely full. The store fronts lined up along both sides of the streets and the signs were all wood carved and handmade matching the next one beside it.

There were two favorite places for me to visit. One was a relatively new store, Anne's Boutique. It opened a few years before, but she carried trendy clothes on consignment, and I could always find something when I would shop while visiting my family—the few times I was able to visit.

The other shop I enjoyed visiting was simply called The General Store. They still sold penny candy, homemade ice cream, and select items normally found in big department stores, such as basic hardware, toys, crafts, and, yes, even sewing material. It was like something displaced from the set of *Little House on the Prairie*.

Doris and Jack Miller have run the place since they were first married in their early twenties. Jack took over the business from his dad who took it over from his. What they sell in that store is not modern by any means but necessary nonetheless. My Dad and Jack were good friends. It was time I paid them a visit.

A bell notified the owners of my arrival. I was surprised to see both standing behind the counter. Immediately Doris' face lit up, and she shuffled to the front and hugged me tightly. Her embrace ended with a loud kiss on the cheek and shake of my shoulders. Jack could see the surprise on my face and settled for a gentleman's bow and kiss on my hand, "My lady," he said in his best prince voice.

"How are you two doing?" I said leaning over the glass display case and resting my forearms on the list of ice cream choices.

Doris laid her hands on mine. "Darling, we keep kicking and ticking. Nothing stops us, you know."

"You've changed the displays over there." I pointed to where shelving that held pottery once stood. Now there were four-ways of hanging t-shirts for sale.

Jack was first to answer. "Why Ms. Pam, you are an observant child. Yes. These are new for us. We're hoping the young crowd finds us."

"I'm sure they will," I encouraged them.

"So what brings you by, dear?" Doris asked.

There was a question that I knew she would have an answer to, "Can you tell me about the library? I hear they are hiring for a position there."

Jack left her side to carry a box to the back while she answered, "You haven't heard? Mrs. Grayson passed away, a few months or so ago. Well maybe it was even before the New Year," she stopped to think, "Yeah I remember it was in the winter. Anyway, that position has been open for a long time… you should…"

She kept talking, but I didn't hear her. I focused on my memory, to just a month ago, when I stopped in for a visit. *She was there. I saw her. I talked with her. Didn't I?*

Doris saw my skin pale and my eyes drift. "Are you okay dear?"

I shook my head and swallowed.

She led me to a small booth by the window where customers sat to enjoy their ice cream. I sank down into the seat and felt my arms grow heavy. A coldness came over me. I thought I was going to faint.

Chapter Sixty-Eight

"Only volunteers have run the library since she passed away. But that place was her life. She stayed there all hours of the day. Since she retired from the school that library was her second—no, make that her first home. Mr. Grayson died while she was still a teacher, and both her sons moved away years ago. There was nothing left but those books for her. So if any place around here was haunted with a spirit, it was surely gonna be that library and by Mrs. Grayson's ghost."

By now I had a cup of water in front of me and had mostly recovered from the verge of passing out. I was listening to Doris tell her haunted library story. It was still too hard to understand what I witnessed.

I convinced myself that I was either dreaming about visiting or about the person I talked to the day I went to the library. I excused myself and headed back toward the library. I was going to see which one was the right answer and more importantly to prove to myself that I wasn't going crazy.

But the sign on the door read *'Temporarily Closed—For Emergencies Call Trish'* with a phone number. I stood facing the door and dialed the number. I received a voicemail. I left a message. "Hi Trish, This is Pam Taylor. I was interested in applying for the position at the library. I came by but saw the closed sign. Please call me and let me know when a good time would be to stop back by. Thank you."

I hadn't even made it back to my parents' house before the phone in my pocket rang. "Hello?"

"Pam? It's Trish. I am *so* happy you called. Yes, we need someone desperately. Tomorrow is Thursday, right? I can be there at nine in the morning if you would like to stop in," she said eagerly.

"I'll be there!" I said and smiled at my phone as she said goodbye and hung up. This job-hunting thing might be easier than I thought.

Chapter Sixty-Nine

Thursday morning I pulled into the library parking lot as Trish was opening the front door with a key she fought to hold with her right key while balancing a stack of magazines under her left arm. She smiled and nodded her head in my direction as she pushed forward inside. I ran ahead to help her with the load she was carrying. She threw her keys on the counter and dropped the remaining items while holding her hand out to shake mine as she took a deep breath.

"I'm Trish," she said.

"Pamela. Pam. It's nice to meet you." I shook back.

She tilted her head toward me. "You look familiar."

"I grew up here. My Mom and Dad actually still live across the street. The Taylors."

She shook her head slightly. "I don't know them. I married someone from this area, so I don't know a lot of the locals. Anyway, come in to the office. Have a seat."

I put the folder with my resume on the table and placed my hands in my lap when I sat down. For some reason I was suddenly nervous.

"Listen, I'm not going to waste your time," she said as she made coffee.

My heart sank.

"Wait, before you say anything. I was here a few months ago." I paused remembering the odd conversation with Doris the day before. "I really think this is a perfect place for me to put down roots. I have a degree in history. I have a relatively strong resume. I am dependable. I've moved back and live close by now."

"That's it! You came in here not that long ago. I was on the phone back here in the office. I saw you out there. You looked like you might have been talking to someone, maybe on the phone. When I came out you were gone. I knew I saw you before." She was proud of the memory resurfacing for her.

I just smiled and nodded wondering if it was appropriate to ask if a place was haunted during an interview.

She interrupted my thoughts. "No, I completely understand that you are available, and it sounds like you are qualified—probably overly qualified to work in a small community library like this. I just think that you should understand that it can be too quiet here. Sometimes your imagination can even make things up to pass the time between customers—but we really need someone, and we need someone fast."

"Well, I'm here, and I'm ready. I'm someone." I laughed.

She looked at me with curious eyes and chewed the side of her cheek. She nodded twice and continued. "Okay, I think you'd be perfect."

"Wonderful. I—"

She stopped me. "Wait. There's just one catch. I kinda need you to start right now. As you can see, there is a lot to do around here." She drew her arm around to show the piles of books that were neglected around her.

"Now? You mean, like, today?"

Trish nodded with a look of utter need.

"And this?" I showed her my resume.

"No need. We'll work out the paperwork details later."

"Okay then. Let's do this!" I said, pushing my chair back and standing to shake her hand one more time.

I rolled up my sleeves to dig in.

Chapter Seventy

Mrs. Grayson didn't talk to me while I worked that day. In fact, the library seemed too quiet at times. I began to wonder if I made a mistake taking that job. If this was how most days would be I might go crazy with the lack of sound. But then, the more I thought about it, the more I could get used to the peace and being able to manage my thoughts.

I was still thinking about Mrs. Grayson that afternoon while I fixed dinner and even while I was putting the dishes into the dishwasher. I didn't know who I could talk to about her or even if I wanted to talk about her. It was bad enough Doris and Jack heard my story. What I wanted to do was pretend like I had not seen nor spoke with her. At all.

These thoughts swam around my already-full head as I looked around the living room. Both girls were crowding the couch, piled high with pillows, laptops, cell phones, and earbuds with music piping directly through their ears. Dad was laid back on his recliner, fighting sleep as he watched a crime show. Mom had eaten with us, quietly now that she was on her new medicine. She had retreated back to her bedroom. I shook my head. Mrs. Grayson was better company than them. I had to get out of there.

I decided to go to my new Thursday hang-out—the place where people actually communicated. That evening I walked to the grief meeting at Grace Church. I chuckled to myself as I thought about how much I was looking forward to it. The other attendees had given me hope they didn't even know they offered. In the little pieces that were just small parts of their big stories is where I found the help I needed.

A middle-aged woman, whose name I couldn't recall at the

moment, had mentioned her healing involved going back to work and getting a routine in place. This was one of the reasons I decided to apply to the opening at the library. I needed a routine; a normal, same ol' boring routine. The kind I complained about just months before.

As I maneuvered around two kids on skateboards, I knew I couldn't lie to myself. Listening to the other attendees for advice was not the only reason for my wanting to go tonight. I was also looking forward to seeing Travis. The heat from the day was still radiating off the pavement beside me. I used that as the reason for why I was suddenly getting so warm.

Chapter Seventy-One

He didn't show. I watched the door all night, fighting the nerves as my stomach danced each time the distinct screech of the door sliding over the frame was heard from my left.

I barely paid attention to anything that was said, so whatever benefit my being there was, left with the unknown. People began to converse at the end of the meeting, but I left before anyone else, disappointment flowing through my entire being, and I was upset at myself for letting it get to me.

What was I thinking? I asked myself on the walk home. *He didn't get captured by aliens and removed from the planet. At least I didn't think he did. This is something Presley would be stressing over. He's just another boy.* I laughed at that thought. I'd see him soon enough. Maybe even the next day as that was the one he suggested for our date. My heart began to race at the very thought of that.

I silently thought, *This is a new millennium, and there is modern technology to keep us in touch. I told him to call me. And he will. Even if he doesn't, the phone went both ways. I can call him anytime to talk to him.* I told myself that it was okay for a woman to do that. I shook my head and allowed the argument to continue in my head until I walked through the front door.

With the exception of mom having joined them and empty popcorn bowls on the coffee table, everyone was as I had left them. Their eyes were glued to the television as an action movie blared though the surround sound. Nobody looked my way or acknowledged the front door had even opened. *This family would fall apart without me,* I thought as I walked past them to take a shower.

Seeing my phone on the nightstand as I gathered my pajamas I again thought about calling him. I even picked it up and started to page through my contacts. I had to remind myself that even though it had been a while since I dated or even communicated with someone of the opposite sex that wasn't my father, the phone did go both ways.

No, there must have been a reason for him missing the meeting tonight. I knew the importance that group had for him, so whatever it was had to be important. I didn't want to bother him. As if realizing the phone was a ticking time bomb, I heaved it into the stack of pillows on the bed. It landed face down on the comforter.

Had it been right side up, I would have seen the screen light up and the name *Travis* flash across the front. Instead it vibrated quietly and unnoticed into the mattress, and I walked to the bathroom in a cloud of defeat.

Chapter Seventy-Two

I was truly the worst person to check missed calls and messages on my phone. The girls were always yelling at me about it, so it was no exception that it wasn't until I was walking into the library at lunch time the following day for my afternoon shift that I even noticed a voice message alert on my phone.

I immediately called him back.

Since it was mid-day I hoped to catch his voice mail, praying he'd be in with a patient. I was wrong. Before I could even say hello, he was laughing on the other end.

"Wow. Only sixteen hours late on a return call. Could be worse, I guess," he finally said.

"I'm so, so sorry," I found myself cringing and explained my poor habit of not noticing messages.

Before I could finish, he stopped my apology, asking me what I should have seen coming but was blindsided nonetheless. He asked me on a first official date. *Official. Date.* Not the friendly diner just to get something to eat on our way to a grievance meeting, but one that I could be dressed up for, and it was set for that evening.

"I was hoping to be able to do it in person at the meeting last night, but I couldn't get there. I wanted to give you a day's notice. I know how you ladies are."

This time *I* laughed. "Us ladies, Huh? Where exactly are you taking me that would require twenty-four hours of prep time?"

"Let's just say it will require a little drive to get there."

After hanging up with him, I was no longer able to concentrate at work. Trish mentioned Fridays were busy days, but as visitors stopped in to get on computers or check out and return books, I found myself more often than not drifting off into a daydream. As the last mother and daughter stood browsing young adult books in the back corner of the library, I busied myself with checking books back into the system.

My peripheral vision caught something light in color move to my right, toward the office. I got up from the stool and went to investigate. I could still hear the people in the back talking quietly. It wasn't them. I went inside the office, but there was nobody there. It didn't matter that I couldn't see her. I knew she was there.

"Good Afternoon, Mrs. Grayson. No need to worry. If you're here to check on me, it's okay. I'm taking care of the library." I turned to walk back to the computer. "Oh, but you're welcome to stay here and keep me company as long as you'd like."

Chapter Seventy-Three

Presley answered the door when Travis arrived. She was listening to her music, earbuds in, and didn't say a word when she motioned him in.

Kennedy stood from the kitchen stool and came around the corner to say hello. "She's been in the bedroom for over an hour. I'm sure she's almost done. I'll go let her know you're here."

"Thank you," Travis replied. He walked toward the couch where Mom sat. She immediately recognized him.

"Doctor Travis? You make house calls now?" she asked while straightening her robe.

He patted her forearm as he sat. "I'm off the clock Mrs. Taylor. No working for me. But it's great to see you awake and recognizing me."

"Of course I know you. Why wouldn't I know you?" she huffed sarcastically.

Travis patted her arm again for reassurance before standing.

As he did, I came down the hall. He was in a sport coat and dress pants. He was so handsome. I, on the other hand, felt awkward in heels and a dress. I can't remember the last time I went on a fancy date, let alone dressed up for one.

He turned as my heels clicked on the hardwood. His mouth and eyes opened as if pulled on with strings.

"Pam. Wow!" The only two words I needed to hear.

"Hi Travis." I hugged him and looked around at the others watching me, everyone but Presley was smiling. She was engrossed in her music. "Are you ready?" I asked.

"Yes ma'am," he said as he opened the door and lightly guided me with the palm of his hand on my back.

I was surprised at his car. An early '90s BMW. And it was dirty with a dent in the front fender and rust on the bumper. "Your car is… lovely," I noted as we walked down the sidewalk.

"No, it's not. But I'm a cheap bachelor. Plus, I only use it to go back and forth from the hospital. I did try to wash it, and I vacuumed and cleaned most of the inside." He opened the door for me. "That's the part that counts, right?"

"It's perfect." I smiled.

Chapter Seventy-Four

Our date started with Travis driving east into the city thirty-five miles away. With probably twenty large household name establishments in the area he could have chosen from to take me to, I was surprised when he pulled into a lonely alleyway where a man in white button down and black pants took his keys to valet his car. I looked around. There weren't any cars around. I silently wondered where he took it to park. Shaking that thought from my head I simply took his extended arm and walked with Travis through the canopied entrance. The place we went to for dinner was small, classy, and quiet. The dining area was no larger than the average home's living room, making it very romantic. Airy '50s music was piped softly into the room and each table was lit by candlelight under dim ambient lighting. It was remarkable. I never knew places like this even existed off the movie screen. The service and food were equally phenomenal.

Over glasses of red wine, delicious food, and finally pie and coffee we spent almost three hours talking about everything we could think of besides sick patients and the hospital. Even though Travis knew Kennedy and Presley, I told him more about who they were. I talked about my past jobs and getting hired on at the library. I even confessed how I thought I was sharing the space with a potential ghost. He told me about his love of reading, carpentry as a hobby, and how he started to write a novel that he'd one day love to finish.

Conversation went so smoothly between the two of us that the evening sailed by. We moved the date outside and walked the sidewalk around the block. When we ran out of concrete, Travis faced me and interrupted my story of how my girls almost caught the kitchen on fire making me breakfast in bed one Mother's day.

Then, as if in slow motion he stole a kiss. He moved so quickly that his hands were on my face tilting my head up to meet his, and before I knew it my words trailed off, and my arms were firmly wrapped around his back. It was minutes before he pulled away.

"I'm so sorry," he finally apologized. "I would like to say that I couldn't stop staring at your lips or that I didn't just forget what you were talking about, but I can't. I just had to—"

"No, don't apologize. That was… perfect. Again. I know, like your car, like this night… I need to expand my vocabulary."

He shook his head. "No, you are… well, you are perfect too."

Holding hands, we walked back to the valet stand to retrieve the car. He drove me home with more light conversation and quickly kissed me good-bye. He left me with a promise to call me soon.

After that first date night, I spent the next two and half weeks going on three more dates and talking to Travis seven, no eight times on the phone. I also took care of mom as she rode a roller coaster on her new medication and pacified a discouraged Presley while keeping Kennedy motivated for her voluntary double-shifts at work. It was an exhausting few weeks to say the least. But as I laid down after all that I couldn't help but smile. A year ago I never would have thought I would be living with my parents, taking care of one of them, and no longer working in my executive position. My life was certainly different.

Twice as different.

Chapter Seventy-Five

I began to think everything was falling into place in our life. Finally we were developing a routine. The girls had their jobs. I had mine. Mom was doing better on her medication. The doctor visits were becoming fewer and were more for maintenance than a requirement. And speaking of the doctor, our relationship was beginning to truly bloom. It was starting to feel normal in my life. Travis and I began to see each other regularly, even doing things with the entire family.

So, how could I have been so blindsided?

Nothing could have prepared me for the next two days.

It was a Thursday morning. Having spent a late night with Travis after the grief meeting, I slept in, waking for work at nine o'clock. I wanted to be to the library by ten even though we didn't open until lunchtime. Before leaving, I looked in on the girls. I don't know why I did, but that morning I wanted to make sure they were okay. Both were sound asleep. I knew they had both worked late the night before, but their synchronized deep breathing meant sleeping in would be a welcome change for them.

I quietly pulled the door shut and said goodbye to my dad who was reading the paper in the kitchen. He was sipping his coffee cup, which I assumed was at least his third one that morning. I heard Mom getting ready in her bathroom whose wall backed up to mine. It was nice to know she was getting back on a regular schedule like the rest of us.

Work was quiet that day. There was a puppet show local teenagers put on for the children in the area, and then I reorganized periodicals along the front wall for the rest of the day. Before I knew it five o'clock had arrived.

My phone rang in the bottom of my purse, and I fished for it as I tried to lock up. By the time I pulled it out and answered the call had ended. It was Kennedy. Walking back toward the house I tried to call her again, this time her phone went to voice mail. Knowing I'd be home within minutes I pocketed the phone, readjusted my cross-body purse, and headed home.

As I hit the front steps my phone rang again.

"Mom, where are you?" Kennedy asked breathlessly before I could say hello.

"Kennedy—I'm right here on the porch."

"Good! We need you."

"What's wrong? Is grandma okay?" I opened the door and practically burst into the house.

Mom, Dad, and Kennedy were all standing in the living room. Mom had her arms wrapped around herself with a scared look. Dad's eye brows were creased, but it was Kennedy who was most concerned; her eyes wide as she hung up her phone.

"Where's Presley?" I looked around, accounting for three of four people that should have been there.

Chapter Seventy-Six

"She's not here," my dad answered.

"Where'd she go? I mean the car's out there. Did she walk to town?" I asked.

He shook his head.

Mom rocked back and forth.

Kennedy started crying.

Fear began to bubble inside me. "Okay. Where is she?"

Kennedy looked up with tears welled in her eyes. "We don't know."

"What do you mean you *don't know?*"

She handed me a folded up page of notebook paper.

I swallowed hard and opened it up. It read:

"Kenn

I'm leaving this on your bedside table because I'd rather tell you than anyone else. Don't worry I'm not running away but I'm certainly not staying here. I hate this place. How can you possibly stand it? I'm not stupid. I have a plan so I'll be okay. Plus I have Nate. He said I could stay with him. I told you about him, remem? Anyway, I'll call you when I get settled. Love you sis.

Always!! xoxo

Pres"

"Kennedy. Who is Nate?" I asked before I even looked up from the paper.

"Mom. I honestly have no idea. She mentioned a guy… I think his name could have been Nate. I know she texted someone a lot. It must have been him, but I've been too busy to really pay attention to her latest boyfriend. I'm so sorry. I know I should—"

I stopped her. "No. You shouldn't. You shouldn't have to babysit her. When did you find this?"

"Just now. When I woke up it was almost eleven. She was gone. I thought she was just out. I don't know… By then she could have been long gone."

"No, I looked in on you two this morning before I left. You were both sleeping. Well, I *thought* you were both sleeping. Now I…" I sank into the couch.

I looked at my parents. "Dad did you see her leave? You were in the kitchen."

He shook his head. "I didn't see her. I was looking for a socket wrench in the garage this morning. I guess that's where I was."

"Mom?"

She stopped rocking. "I told her good-bye."

"What! Why didn't you stop her?"

"She said she'd be back. She said she was going to see you." Her eyes fell to the floor.

I ran my hands over my hair and rested them on the back of my neck.

"Mom, what do we do?" Kennedy sobbed.

"We find her."

Chapter Seventy-Seven

I hurried to the kitchen. I was on a mission, but I'm not sure I even knew where I needed to begin. I said the first thing that came to mind, "Kennedy grab your yearbooks and bring them here. Try to remember everyone you can at the old school named Nate or Nathan or even Nathaniel. Dad, call everyone you know working in town. Ask if they know anything. Maybe they saw her walking."

Looking at mom I could see the stress beginning to overwhelm her. The rocking was growing more intense, and her eyes were darting. I grabbed an anxiety pill and bottle of water and then grabbed her in a hug. "Don't worry. She'll be back soon." I handed her the pill and bottle and nodded for her to take it.

She didn't argue.

I walked to the girls' bedroom and passed Kennedy looking through old moving boxes. I began tearing through her bedding and shelves. "Have you called her cellphone?"

"Of course. But it's turned off, goes straight to voicemail."

"Doesn't surprise me. I'm assuming she's already with Nate. He picked her up… wherever. Now she doesn't need her phone on anymore. What about her computer?"

"Good call, Mom." She stood up, a stack of books in her arms. "She usually keeps it under her bed when she's not on it."

Reaching underneath I swiped my arm across the ground, coming in contact with a hard object. Her laptop. I pulled it out and opened it up while simultaneously turning it on. "Use your phone and call her again and bring the books to the kitchen. Our investigation has officially begun."

Chapter Seventy-Eight

Decoding the password into her computer was not difficult. The tricky part was getting into her social media accounts. We tried everything and every combination of words we could think of, eventually we were locked out. I was getting very frustrated and sighed deeply as I leaned my head against the kitchen wall.

In his mission to call people, Dad had gotten in touch with Sheriff Wheaton. The two were friends from decades of sharing the same bleacher row at high school football games on Friday nights. Even though they couldn't technically open a police report until she had been missing for twenty-four hours, he came over, and the two of them were talking in the living room. I would turn my head to listen to them as we tried to log-in. Finally Kennedy had the idea to just use her account and see what she could from our side.

There were cryptic messages on her page. Someone by the name of Star Powers, I assumed an alias, would say numbers or words and Presley would answer in a similar way. For example, one message started with Presley saying *K2G 2 on 3*. The reply from Star was *BBC 2 on 3xo*. And she ended with *LA*.

"Obviously she knew we'd be looking on here. She thinks she's smarter than me. I'm calling the cell phone company. She'll be wishing she was smarter, that's for sure."

"I'll try to figure out what this message means," Kennedy said, glad to help.

The conversation in the living room had turned into friendly banter, laughs, and jokes. Well, I guess their detective work was done for the moment.

I tuned them out and focused on being on hold with the cell-phone company. I was engrossed in the music when, fittingly a customer service representative named Melody came onto the line. Her light and airy demeanor and the long introduction of the latest products and services I should try quickly made my blood boil. "Melody," I interrupted her. "I need to get as much information as I can on the calls and texts placed to and from my daughter Presley Taylor's phone." I gave her the number and verified my email address. She said it would arrive within the next few minutes. As she was asking if I was satisfied with her assistance, I hung up.

Chapter Seventy-Nine

While waiting to receive the phone log Melody promised, I paged through yearbooks with Kennedy. There were a number of Nathans. "None are her type, Mom," Kennedy commented. "She likes jocks—muscles, blond streaked hair, and rarely any intelligence."

The ones we found were on the debate team, marching band, and drama club. They were short, dark-haired, or wearing glasses and sweater vests. All opposites from what she described.

When we got to the basketball team, Kennedy put her hand on mine to stop paging. "That's part of the message. The BBC stands for basketball court. We used to joke that the boys in school were royalty because they played on the BBC. That's where she must have met this Star Powers person."

Looking at the screen on the laptop I agreed. "That's right. The basketball courts are on Third Street. That must be where she went." I gave the information to Sheriff Wheaton.

Sitting back in my seat, I asked out loud, "But who would drive from the old high school to pick her up so far away?"

"I doubt he went to our school. If he did he's probably older." Kennedy propped her chin on her hand.

That was exactly right. He was older. A high school senior would not drive across state to pick up a girlfriend in a borrowed car or with a curfew. This guy was older. Maybe in college, or even out of college. "Ugh." I sank further into the stool as if it could swallow me. I didn't want to think about some older man taking advantage of my daughter. I knew it happened. More often than not. I just thought she was smarter. Or I paid more attention.

As if Kennedy knew I needed her touch, she reached over and

squeezed my forearm. "Don't worry. Presley's the toughest person I know. She'll be okay."

In my heart I believed it, but in my gut… deep down where only mother's feel… I was sick with worry. I knew she was in danger.

Chapter Eighty

Presley had been pressed up against Nate for the entire ride. She held his hand, laid her head on his shoulder, and began to feel her heart grow. She assumed it was love. Her heart jumped when she thought of him, so that is what love was, right? Regardless, she knew it was different with him than with the other boys she'd gone out with.

They connected so deeply with their late night conversations, texts that were hidden under bed covers to shield the screen light. Emails documented day-long events, all ending with terms of endearment longing for more and waiting for this moment.

Plus, Nate was older. He wasn't some kid. He knew what he wanted. The minute he told her he was bringing her back with him to his dorm at college, she knew he must have wanted to take the relationship to a full time level. They had never met. Well not more than a wave across a crowded beach one time; when at Wellington Beach Club for summer fling beach party the year before when she and two of her other friends crashed a high school graduation. His party.

Nate was playing beach volleyball, Presley and her friends were lying on the beach when the ball rolled toward them. Presley had thrown it back, and Nate was the one to nod and wave in appreciation. Her friend knew who he was because her brother had graduated with his class that year. She got his number from the friend, and they texted and messaged off and on since then. It was only when they moved to King Lake when she found herself talking with him regularly. She hadn't talked to any of her other friends from that beach party that day, and now she wondered why Kennedy wasn't with her on that beach trip. She shook the thought from her head and nestled closer into Nate's shoulder.

He smelled so good. She closed her eyes and butterflies danced in her stomach. She took in a deep draw of his scent and smiled. Her mom would understand. When she got to the college she'd call. She'd explain that she would come back before summer was out. By then she'd be too far away for her mom to drive to pick her up. Plus, it was only for a few weeks.

As much as she hated King Lake and the idea of having had to move from the beach, she wouldn't ever hurt her mom or sister. She just wanted to be free, to see her friends again, to put her toes in the sand and feel the waves crash onto her legs once more as the sun painted her skin. She also wanted to see if Old Dominion University was a college for her to possibly attend one day. Her mom and sister couldn't fault her for wanting to start planning her college education early, could they?

Chapter Eighty-One

It was after two in the morning, and I could hardly hold my eyes open. From the tears I fought as I blindly cried, to the pages of three months worth of messages that I'd just received from the cell phone company. I tried all unrecognizable numbers but either they were for a dead end or the number was no longer in service. Any further investigation with the report would be left in the hands of the detectives—if they ever started to work on the case.

My stomach ached from nerves, lack of food, and an overdose of strong coffee. I knew I needed to sleep but felt like in doing so I would miss out on some small detail that needed my attention at that exact moment. Who was I kidding? I couldn't even read the blurred screen let alone focus on any of the details.

In the living room the television was on but muted. Kennedy was on the floor. Her laptop was open, but the screen was asleep—as was she. She was surrounded by a pile of throw pillows, and an old fleece blanket mostly covered her lean frame. I shut the laptop, moving it to the coffee table and switched off the TV.

Throwing my exhausted body face first onto the couch, I knew the only sleep I'd get now was by willing my body to do so. I tried to find a good position on the cushions. After a few rolling attempts I stood up and took each one off the couch to flip them. In doing so a small pink notebook page fluttered out from the side of the last cushion. In girlish handwriting the bubble letters spelled out ODU all over the front and back. I crumpled it up and flopped one last time into position. Much better. That was the final thought I had before sun awoke me for a new day.

Chapter Eighty-Two

Presley was amazed with how clean Nate was for a single guy living by himself. There were no dishes in the sink, no clothes on the floor, but most impressive was the matching dark furnishings and high-end appliances and electronics throughout his apartment. Everything was spotless; in fact everything was brand new. This just confirmed what she thought when he picked her up in the brand new convertible. *He has money.* She was sure that no other freshman at college had life so good. She shyly smiled at the thought and absently ran her hand along the granite counter. He was on his phone on the patio. She was left to explore the apartment by herself. When she got to the bedrooms she froze noting that although there were two rooms only one had a bed—his room.

"He better not think I'm *that* kind of girl," she whispered to herself.

She was admiring the bold artwork in the second bedroom when he walked in.

"Sorry, never a quiet moment in my life," he said meeting her at her side.

Without Presley having to ask, he answered the two questions in her mind. "They came from Ikea. Although not fancy, the room had bare walls just a few weeks ago. We'll try to find another bed there as soon as possible. For now I'll sleep on the couch and you can have the master bedroom."

She smiled at his kindness then hugged him, more for reassurance for herself than gratitude.

His phone rang once more, and he was again out the door to talk on the patio. While he was gone, Presley moved the small duffle bag she brought with her to the master bedroom. She didn't need to unpack. Living as if in a hotel was fine for her for a while. As she waited for him to return she fell onto the bed. The smell of his cologne wafted around her, and she closed her eyes and drank it in. He was gorgeous, generous, and obviously rich. She couldn't think of anything else she'd need to make him more perfect.

As time passed, her stomach started to ache. It must be from lack of food. It was a long drive there with only a few convenience store deli stops along the way.

Pocketing his phone, Nate entered the room and sat on the bed beside Presley. He laid his hand on hers before speaking. "Coach needs me at the gym. He has a roster to go over with me. I need to leave for a few minutes. If you're hungry eat anything you can find or call for take-out from one of menus on the fridg," and as if someone else was listening he leaned over and whispered into her ear, "there is a cookie jar on the counter. There's money in it, not cookies. So help yourself to whatever you need. I shouldn't be long." He kissed her lightly, and with that he was gone, leaving Presley to only smile and nod.

Chapter Eighty-Three

My arm was asleep when I woke the next morning. As I shook it awake, my eyes focused on the cable box clock. 7:42. It was too quiet for that time of the morning. Where was everyone? Looking down I saw Kennedy still asleep on the floor. "That was anything by comfortable," I said to myself.

I sat up and pressed my disheveled hair down with my one working arm.

I heard dad in the kitchen trying not to rattle coffee mugs as he search for his favorite. "Where's Mom?" I asked.

"She's not feeling well. I'm hoping coffee will help," he replied.

"I'll take it to her." I swiped the mug from the counter as I walked past.

Lightly knocking, I pushed the door open at the same time. Mom was sitting up in the bed looking out the window.

"Mom? I brought you some coffee."

She turned and look toward me, taking the mug. "Thank you dear."

"Are you okay?"

"I don't know. I guess. Everything is just foggy. It's like I am constantly trying to remember what I wanted to say or… or, it's like I know a word for a crossword puzzle, but I draw a blank."

I nodded. "Maybe you should call Dr. Hamilton."

"No! I'm not going back to that doctor. He can't fix me. I'm not giving him another dime let alone another chance."

I crossed my arms. "Mom. it's not Trav… Dr. Hamilton's fault you aren't getting better, or you think you aren't getting better. You need time. He isn't a miracle worker."

She took a long drag on her mug before turning to look at me. It was as if she was deep in plans for a plot before she finally spoke again. "You're right. He's *not* a miracle worker. The pills he gave me aren't magic beans. And the time we spent in his office and the hospital isn't something we'll get back. So, because of that, I'm done with him… and the drugs… and the hospital."

"Oh Mother. Do you even listen to yourself?" I shook my head before turning and walking out her door. Although she had now been added to my list, there were other issues I had to deal with before getting to her.

In the living room Kennedy was now awake and sitting on the couch with her knees pulled to her chest and gripping her cell phone.

"You can't will it to ring," I said, pointing to the mess on the floor. "Now pick up all this stuff, we're going to the police station to get the detective motivated to help us."

She started to pick up the pillows and her blanket, and Dad met me in the living room with my cup of coffee.

"Thank you. Mom has picked a bad day to think she can rebel against the medical system." I took the mug from him.

"It's why I suggested she stay in bed today," he said. "Maybe if you give me his number I'll try to…"

"It's okay. I'll call Dr. Hamilton today, after… after everything else."

I flopped onto the couch just as Kennedy was finishing up. "Done. Let me get changed, and I'll be ready to go."

"Wait, you forgot this." I pushed the pink paper I'd found the night before with my toe. "Is it yours?"

"No. What's on it?"

She flattened the paper and examined it. "I have no idea what 'odu' is. It's not mine."

"Well then if it's not yours it must be Presley's. Let's take it with us. Might be worth something."

Chapter Eighty-Four

After sitting on the kitchen stool and staring at the menus from over ten restaurants that deliver to the college, Presley finally decided on Chinese. She hadn't been able to find good sweet and sour chicken since they lived at the beach. It was after 9:30, and she realized she was now starving. Everything looked good on the menu and soon enough she would have over twenty-eight dollars' worth of food coming within thirty minutes or less.

Not knowing the exact address, she stepped outside to look for a number on the building. With the darkened porch she wasn't coming up with any information on the building itself. She thought about the possibility of there being mail in the box by the front door.

There were two advertisements. The one on top said to the *resident* with an address. She gave that number to the person taking her order on the phone and replaced the mail into the box as she hung up. Just as she was making her way back toward the door she heard footsteps running up the walk behind her. Scared, she turned quickly to confront the visitor. A young man with messy blond hair and nice smile stopped in front of Presley.

"Hi. Can I help you?" she offered, politely yet keeping concern in her voice.

"Just looking for Al," he replied. "Have you seen him?"

"Uh, no." She shook her head.

"Well, *humph.* I guess if you see him let him know Jay stopped by."

Presley nodded. More in the comfort of knowing any gesture in the form of agreement would get her back into the house quickly.

Jay nodded, then trotted back down the sidewalk. "See ya."

Presley waved and ducked back inside. She shook off the conversation and sank into the deep mahogany leather sofa, propping her feet on the coffee table and concentrated on learning how to turn on the TV. First, she would have to find out which of the five remotes lined up on the end table was the one for the television.

Chapter Eighty-Five

"What do you mean you still can't help us?" I had remained standing even though Officer Martin asked me to have a seat. "I want to speak with Detective Emerson."

The officer sat back in his brown leather chair reclining it until it let out a long squeaking sound. He clicked his pen in frustration. "I'm sorry Ms. Taylor, he's not in yet. And I've told you that we have to wait at least twenty-four hours. It's what we do in all runaway cases."

Through gritted teeth I repeated my same reply, "That's only a few hours from now and she… is… not… a runaway."

"Ma'am, do you think after leaving a note, like she did that she was taken against her will?"

"Maybe. I wouldn't know for sure. I don't have anyone helping me find her that could *also* help me with that kind of question."

"Runaway cases just don't take priority."

I looked around at the cops with feet propped up, phones silent and computer screens black. Then I ground my teeth until my jaws hurt. "It would if she was yours."

There were prolonged moments of silence as we stared at each other. Finally Officer Martin broke it by picking up his phone. "Let me see where Detective Emerson is."

"Thank you." I finally sank into the chair.

As he dialed I glanced over at Kennedy at the side wall. There was only one chair in the officer's small cubicle. She chose to wait at the side. Now, Kennedy was giving me a questioning look, and I just rolled my eyes and shook my head as if to say, *No use.*

"No answer," the officer said as he hung up.

"But he's coming in today, right?"

He pressed his lips together tightly, raised his eyebrows, and nodded his head.

"Okay, then. We'll wait for him." I pointed. "Over there. In those chairs. Tell me as soon as he gets in."

"Yes Ms. Taylor. I will."

Nodding in silence I got up, maintaining eye contact. What was it with this place? Did everyone not care anymore? Or is that how all police departments were?

While we waited, I called Travis. After letting him know where I was, I apologized for having been distant for a few days. I told him about Mom, how she was acting, and the denial or depressive-like state she seemed to be slipping into.

"Actually, that is pretty normal. This tells me that the medication she is on needs to be tweaked just a little. Again. It's like a dial on a safe, you just keep moving it until it finally clicks. I'll get it called in right away. Just switch it out and start having her take them. The moods should be regulated to a more normal state within a few days."

"Thank you." I sank further into the chair. I needed a little good news to gain momentum for my other situation.

"Do you need me to come over?" he asked, but before I could answer he continued. "I mean I want to be there for you in case you guys need anything. Investigation isn't my specialty, but I have been told I'm a helpful guy, and my shoulders are the perfect size for support. My arms give good hugs too, right?"

I laughed and closed my eyes. "Yes. Actually I'd love for you to come over. I think it would greatly help."

As we said our good-byes a tall figure came into view. His silver hair shone brightly with the morning sun cascading through the main building windows. He removed his sunglasses as he entered and gave a cockeyed smile to the receptionist.

Detective Emerson had finally arrived.

Chapter Eighty-Six

"Ooh, Chinese! My favorite, "Nate exclaimed as he came through the door a little over an hour later. He had seen the to-go containers laid out on the counter."

Presley got up from the couch to meet him. "I know it's late, but I hope you're hungry."

He slid into the first stool he came too. "I'm starving, but not as hungry as you were, I see." He laughed at the mostly empty containers.

"I know. I'm sorry. It's just been a long time since I've had good—I mean *really* good—Chinese."

"That's the thing about college towns. There's a lot of great take-out."

"I bet!" She slid onto the stool to his left and grabbed another piece of broccoli from the cardboard box. She licked her fingers loudly and then nudged him with her shoulder when he gasped.

"Know what's best about it?"

"No. What?" He chewed a mouthful and swallowed before continuing. "They are open almost all night too."

"Chinese at 2 A.M.? Sounds delightful. I'm never leaving now!"

Nate put his arm around Presley and pulled her firmly close to his side. "You'd better not."

After he ate and they cleaned up, he put on a movie and they watched until each fell asleep. As the credits rolled and the screen faded from blue to black and went silent the late night turned into early morning.

Eventually Nate slept reclined where he sat with his feet propped on the table in front of the couch, and Presley used a small throw pillow to lie at the other end of the couch with her feet on his lap.

They slept soundly until the shrill of Nate's phone woke them with a start. It was 8:30 the next morning.

<h1 style="text-align:center">Chapter Eighty-Seven</h1>

Detective Emerson patiently reviewed every page in the file. While he studied and wrote in silence, Kennedy and I exchanged worried looks. My knee bounced causing the table that I rested my elbows on causing it to shake. The detective looked at me over the top rim of his reading glasses as if to silently tell me to stop.

"Sorry." I controlled myself and slid back into my chair.

"Mom," Kennedy whispered.

I was staring at the file trying to read upside down.

Kennedy elbowed me.

I squinted. What time did that say on the report?

"Mom?"

I don't even think that report was filled out completely. Did they even want to help me?

"Mom!" She was louder this time, and it shook me back to the moment.

"What is it?"

She handed me a wrinkled paper. "This."

It was the notebook page we found that morning on the floor, the one I tossed from the couch the night before. I opened it up and studied it while the detective jotted down a few more sentences.

I hadn't noticed the fine border that was creatively added to the paper. It said N8N8N8N8 all around the page. *Nate.* It had taken a long time to add the perfectly centered letters around the edge. In my mind I saw Presley talking with this boy on the phone while she doodled her code name for him. The 'ODU' must be something related to Nate.

"Detective Emerson?" I sat forward with my arm extended.

He looked over his glasses again. He focused on what I had but still didn't say anything.

"I think you should look at this. I think it's important and could be the answer to where we'll find Presley."

Chapter Eighty-Eight

Nate was talking on his phone again on the patio. He was trying to whisper which peaked Presley's interest. She was more awake now and focused her hearing on his conversation.

"Richmond?" he exclaimed in a whispered voice. "Why today?"

"No. No. No, it's okay. I just wish it could wait."

He shuffled dry leaves around on the concrete with his feet. They were probably left there from the fall months before.

"Fine. I'll be there as soon as I can." He hung up as he opened the sliding glass door.

After seeing Presley sitting up he quickly apologized. "I'm so sorry. I tried not to wake you."

She shyly smiled. "It's okay." But curiosity peaked and she asked, "What's in Richmond?"

He stopped walking and looked down at the phone in his hand as if the answer would appear. "Oh, that. Well… it's just… coach has some pads and equipment to drop off at a community college up that way. We are loaning it to them until their grant comes through."

"Oh. Okay. And you have to go? With them?"

"No. I have to go to the office to work on the schedules and roster for the fall camp. And with the gym being open for workouts this summer, we can't leave the place unattended. I told him yesterday I'd fill in if he was going up there. Just didn't think it would be so soon."

"Ahh. So, another day alone, huh?" She couldn't hide her disappointment.

Nate was by her side in two steps. His arms brought her close to his chest. "I promise. As soon as I get back, you'll be all mine. And you have my number so call any time you need me, okay?"

She swallowed hard and forced a smile. What should have

sounded ideal to a new relationship surprisingly made her slink back with concern. She hugged him back, but unknown worry began to invade her conscience. Presley knew letting him go to the athlethic office was what she needed to do, so she didn't let him see her emotions. She needed space to clear her mind.

"I think I'll take a walk around the campus while you're gone. See what's all out there. If I'm thinking of coming here next year, I need to know what's around."

He looked in her eyes holding her gaze a moment before speaking. "I think that's a perfect idea. I'm gonna take a quick shower."

With that he kissed her forehead and turned toward the hallway.

Presley fell back onto the couch and closed her eyes trying to will herself back to sleep. Unable to relax, she decided to just get up and get ready for her walk.

Chapter Eighty-Nine

The campus was beautiful. The grass was so lucious Presley found herself fighting the urge to roll around on the ground just to see if it was as velvety soft as it looked. The students she passed were friendly, and the buildings along the walkway were majestic and clean.

The entire walk was over five miles around the campus as each department and the student housing was laid out equally around the quad. Even though this school was a smaller four-year university it held a prestige all on its own. She didn't need a fancy state school on her academic record, and Old Dominion could be a perfect fit for her. Then, she and Nate could live together full time and their relationship could blossom even more. She smiled at the thought and picked up the pace. Joy put a bounce in her footsteps, and she felt freer than she had since their journey together began.

Passing by the admissions building she decided to backtrack and entered the double doors through which a couple were coming out. She thanked them for holding the door, and they smiled, telling her that it was their pleasure. Again, the politeness was abundant.

A middle aged woman greeted her at the welcome desk. "We're so happy to have you visit us at Old Dominion. How may I assist you?"

"Good morning. I'd like to get some information on possibly attending next year." Presley rested her arms on the desk.

The woman pulled out a blue folder from the top drawer of her desk. "Most certainly! Everything you need is in here. Go ahead and take it with you. The application's in there as well."

"Wow, that was easy. Thank you."

"No problem. And here's a business card with my number if you have questions. "I hope to see you next year."

"Me too." Presley turned to leave.

She couldn't wait to tell Nate about her walk and the admissions visit. She held the folder tight to her chest and walked faster. Maybe he'd be home before too long, and she'd show him. For now she couldn't wait to go through the catalog and papers she was given.

She passed the mail carrier on the way in and remembered she was going to tell Nate the story about using the junk mail to get the Chinese food delivered the day before. Instead she stopped and reached into the box pulling the envelopes and flyers out and thought she'd just lay it on the counter for him when he got home. As she entered through the door the name above the address on the top envelope caught her eye. Al Nathanson. Then, the brief conversation with the blond guy reentered her thoughts. *Al*. Maybe he was an old roommate.

As she sorted through the other mail it too had this Al person's name on it.

She quickly opened drawers and cabinets looking for something else with his name. Coming up with nothing she put the thought out of her mind, settled on a can of cola from the fridge, and decided to read the school newspaper at the table.

Chapter Ninety

With Nate gone unusually long that second time, Presley sat on the wooden dining room chair and stared out the window at the open lawn that was the main courtyard for the college campus. She couldn't concentrate on the paper she tried to read. Who was Al Nathanson? Could that actually be her Nate? Nate Alexander?

It was at that moment when the gravity of what she had just done hit her. She lowered her head, closed her eyes tightly, and took a deep breath, holding it as long as she could. What was she thinking? Did she know Nate from the next guy? She thought she did.

They had talked for a few hours a day over two months now and sent brief messages to each other since the beach party the summer before. Pictures texted and emails sent were what their entire relationship was made up. But two weeks ago he told her he was falling in love with her. And she practically burst with excitement because she had wanted to tell him long before that.

Now, sitting here, it felt like a pit of sinking quicksand coming up around her. She just left her family. She told herself it was because she needed to get back to Wellington Beach, to her friends and her life there. But that would mean leaving Nate here at college just as they were supposed to start a relationship together. But she wasn't out of high school yet.

What would she do for her last year in school? Of course she'd go back to King Lake. She couldn't enroll in school here or back at Wellington Beach. But leaving Nate would be hard. She was trying to get to know him. Would a few weeks be enough time to do that? And Kennedy. What about her twin? She needed her sister. Her heart began to race. She really had run away. She realized it now. Her mom would be so mad at her. She couldn't call. But she couldn't stay here.

She'd just tell Nate she needed to go back. That she made a mistake. But then he would hate her. She couldn't lose him. But she didn't even know him. Was he Al Nathanson? If so, then he lied about his name. Or was he lying to everyone else and had told her the truth?

Everything was getting dizzy, and she felt faint. She put her head between her knees as her mom taught her years ago. As she waited for the darkness to pass and her heart to stop racing, tears welled up in her eyes and streamed steadily down her cheeks. She was scared, sad, confused, and mad. Putting her finger on one emotion was too difficult. She sat up and was immediately overcome with claustrophobia.

She didn't want to think about it anymore. She needed fresh air. And she needed to get outside. Running across the apartment she grabbed her purse. She no longer thought of the bag of clothes still packed on the spare room floor nor did she remember the cookie jar of money she could take with her. Fumbling with the doorknob she yanked as hard as she could and flew through the open frame, colliding into the broad chest of a six foot tall, fifty-something sheriff's deputy with his hand raised to knock. Immediately his arms caught and embraced Presley, and then everything went black.

Chapter Ninety-One

Travis was sitting silently with me on the couch when I got the call. Nobody in the house had talked for the past couple hours. Kennedy was sleeping with her head on my lap, and I mindlessly stroked her hair. I kept brushing it behind her ears and followed the long strands over her shoulder, repeating the gesture hundreds of time without realizing my actions.

To my left, Travis gave me a reassuring squeeze on the leg. I sadly smiled in his direction. I was about to thank him for the third time for being there when the shrill of my cell phone jerked me to attention. The caller ID showed it was the detective. I wanted to answer, but I didn't want bad news. So I stared through three rings before answering, allowing my voice to catch up to my mind. "Hello?" I croaked.

The detective didn't hesitate. He also didn't want to scare us as they did in movies with the, *They've found her* or *I have news*. He simply said, "She's sitting in the sheriff's office outside Norfolk. She was at Old Dominion University. Just as you thought, that paper you gave me was the clue to finding her."

"Thank you," was all I could say.

As I looked around all eyes were now on me, even my mom's, who for the first time in a long time appeared to have real emotion showing on her face, concern for the granddaughter we had lost.

I told them all where she was, and within minutes Travis, Kennedy, and I were in the car heading back east, the same roads we took routinely while visiting my parents. This time the miles of highway seemed longer than usual.

Chapter Ninety-Two

I admit that I was speeding most of the way. In just under seven hours I was pulling into the parking lot of the sheriff's office. Presley met me at the door and grabbed me into her arms, knocking the breath from me. Tears poured from her eyes, and as if she was again a toddler I let her cry it out while I held her. By now Kennedy had met us, and she too wrapped her arms around us.

"It's okay. We're here now," I whispered into her hair.

She repeatedly told me she was sorry, and I just shook my head to let her know it was okay. Sheriff Barkley introduced himself, and I let go of Presley long enough to embrace and thank him as well. "I've never been happier to be part of this department than I was the moment I found… or actually Presley ran into me… literally," he laughed. "Would you mind coming into my office to complete some forms?"

"Of course." I nodded for the girls to join Travis in the car, who had now moved into the driver's seat. Quickly, I followed Sheriff Barkley inside.

When seated, he scribbled on a paper in an open file and slid it over in front of me. He didn't move his hand though before talking, "She's lucky Ms. Taylor."

I didn't answer just looked back at him with the pen suspended."

"The boy she was staying with—well to put it bluntly, he's bad news."

"What? Are you kidding? What did you find out?" I could feel anger and fear both well into my cheeks as the emotions crept up my neck.

"Nate, or should I say Al—which is his real name. Has used the alias of Nate in the past to seduce girls, mostly just into his bedroom, but there is one such case that is still waiting to be tried where a young girl claimed to be assaulted while at his apartment. And if that's not bad enough, we were this close—he held his forefinger and thumb a fraction of an inch apar—"to catching him in the act of dealing drugs. We've been working with Norfolk State and Campus Police departments by sending in undercover agents. We had one there today. He, along with the call from King Lake, brought us to Presley. Take her home Ms. Taylor. She's a good girl. She'll be just fine."

And with that I started to cry like I was a toddler.

Chapter Ninety-Three

Presley slept most of the way home. She had cried herself into hysterics, and I had given her a sleep aid to help calm her before leaving the Sheriff's station. Her emotions and the medication had her laying her head on the window frame with her mouth agape. Her eyes were still swollen from tears. Beside her Kennedy was curled with her head on her sister's shoulder, also in deep slumber.

I watched the two of them, finally at peace, without worry and in much needed sleep, and prayed to God thanking Him for the safe return of my daughter. I whispered an *Amen* after promising to never take a moment with them for granted ever again.

Travis, driving beside me, laid his hand on my leg for encouragement. He turned it over, palm up and waited for me to take it. I gladly did and then laid my head on his shoulder. I wasn't tired even though it was well into the night by now. I just watched the lines pass around us in the depth of darkness. We were the only people on the road for miles around.

After a few minutes, I giggled and looked up at him.

"What could possibly be funny?" he asked giggling himself.

"This. You and me. I never pictured this as being part of our relationship. I mean… any relationship." I stumbled, looking for appropriate words.

"Well it certainly will be something to tell the grandkids someday."

I laughed. "And I thought I was jumping the gun by mentioning the word *relationship*."

He looked over at me for a brief second before commenting. "Pam, I couldn't ask for anything more. A relationship with you, your girls, your parents. It's perfect. This is something I've wanted since the day you walked into the hospital. You are amazing. Beautiful.

Caring. And a great mother. So this—all this that seems so busy and overwhelming. Well it's perfect to me… so I'd take it anyway that it came."

I smiled at him and whispered, "Thank you." I couldn't say another word through tears that built in my eyes and voice. Then I simply laid my head back down on Travis' shoulder, and I too eventually drifted off to sleep holding his hand tightly and willing him never to let go.

Chapter Ninety-Four

My world was finally calming down. The swift turning on the axis we'd gone through these past few months was grinding to a slow rotation as good news finally began to come my way. The Friday after arriving back at the house with a newly thankful Presley, Travis gave the family even more good news. Mom's new regimen of medication had regulated her memory, and her manic outbursts had all but disappeared. She recognized everyone in the family, although long term memories were slow at reappearing. Travis believed she would regain more with time. Personally, I knew she was getting back to her old self with the petty remarks she would make about my parenting skills or the meals that I would make. What would irritate me in the past made me thank God for what He did to give me my mom back.

But I knew I could not live forever in a house with her. It wouldn't be healthy for any of us.

This became very apparent after wiping the counter with a cloth I assumed was for the kitchen.

"*Pamela Jean.*" I heard over my shoulder, causing me to jump.

I looked around at what was in front of me and what caused her to yell before turning to see what she needed.

"That is one of my washcloths from the spare bathroom! Why are you using it in the kitchen?"

I apologized and promised to wash it with the next load.

She walked off and sank loudly into the couch cushion with a sigh.

After shaking my head, I picked up my cellphone from the counter and scrolled through the contacts until I found the one I needed. I texted two sentences to Bonnie. "I need your help. Find me a place to live that is *not* with my parents."

She immediately called me. "Oh Lord, tell me you haven't killed anyone!"

I walked out the backdoor sliding it shut behind me. "Of course not—well, not yet."

She laughed, and based on the sound I could tell she was cutting something up. Then I heard a crisp bite. An apple. Her favorite snack. It was that detail that made me realize how much I missed my friend.

"Something's got you angry," she said between bites.

"I have found that even with her condition, I can't live with my mom. Helping her I can do. Living with her, no. No. No. No. I'll need a decade of therapy and have to suffer though countless nights of bad dreams now just thinking about it." Then I told her about Presley running away. "The girls and I need to be a family—alone. Like before."

"I completely get you, but I can't do much as far as showing you places, lady. I'm a little far away, but I'll get you information on anywhere you find. Even a Realtor's name in the area if you'd like."

"Actually, I have one even easier for you to help me with. The library I work at has an apartment above it. It's been vacant for years. Can you help me find the owner of the building?" I told her the address and all the information that I knew. "I've got plans for that place. I'm going to make it our new home."

Chapter Ninety-Five

I love my life. I've finally come to realize this with the time I now have to look in at it. We've been in the apartment for a month now. Even though there were three bedrooms, the girls wanted to share one, so the other room I've made into my own library. How ironic that we have two in the same building. I designed a make shift window seat out of some old cushions and a bench that was left by the owner. Now, as I sit with my coffee watching the girls leave for their first day of their senior year, laughing together no less, I know that I am truly blessed and just plain happy. Period.

Travis and I had now truly dated for three months, and we spend every waking hour together, well aside from our jobs. If he didn't bring dinner to the house, we would cook it together. The girls were working a lot at their jobs, but they were also always with us when they could be. It was a welcome change, especially having a happy Presley around.

Today Travis brought breakfast by on his way into the office. I knew it was out of his way. He didn't care. That is why I love him. I had told him so last night.

I had been very nervous the entire time we walked around the mall. I needed to find a comforter for my new bed, and he claimed to have wanted shoes even though he never once tried them on. As we held hands and walked, there was a long moment of silence between us. I wanted to say something, but everything running through my mind was boring or old news, something we'd already watered down with other conversation, so I found myself blurting out my feelings. He stopped and looked at me, smiling until his cheeks reddened. Then he hugged me, and I apologized for being a sap. An old crazy sap. But he only hugged me tighter. Then in a whisper into my hair he answered me back. "I love you too Pam. And always have."

Chapter Ninety-Six

The date of February 15th will never be forgotten. That was the day Travis proposed to me. The evening before he had a romantic Valentine's dinner catered to my apartment. The girls stayed at my parents' house and it was the most romantic evening I've ever experienced. In fact the most romantic of movies didn't have anything on the plans that he executed to make it the best Valentine's Day a girl could ask for. And he admits that it was a perfect opportunity to propose. Too perfect. And too predictable. I certainly wasn't expecting it, but nonetheless he wanted the right moment to be a complete surprise. He certainly did it, and I didn't have to wait long for him to pull it off.

He had to work the next day but mentioned coming by to check out a book when he got off work. It was my late evening, so I was happy he'd be stopping in to see me. When he came he brought in one to return. All of the behavior was normal. He'd check out the latest medical mystery from his favorite author from time to time. This time he handed me a different book, one that wasn't recognizable to me. It was a small green leather-bound hardcover book without a title on the front. I opened it up to scan the bar code inside and saw it was a journal. I looked up at Travis, and he smiled shyly at me.

"Turn to the bookmark," he said.

I did as he said, and the page read in his handwriting:

"It's been the best year of my life. Work has been rough. Yeah, it's been hard, but my work brought me the best gift I could ask for. She made this past year wonderful, the present even more than I could ever deserve, and now it is time that I ask for my future…"

I looked at him again, and he pulled out a small velvet box, opened it, and the shimmer of a diamond sparkled under the fluorescent lighting. My hands immediately dropped the book on the desk and flew to my mouth covering the gasp I made.

"You are my future, Pam. I can't imagine another day without you in it." He walked around the counter and dropped to one knee. "Complete my dream. Please marry me."

I couldn't find the words, so I just nodded furiously in his direction. Finally able to speak, I said *Yes* over and over and reached out with my left hand while he slid the ring on my finger.

That day, that moment, with happy tears and stunned silence and all was better than any Valentine's Day proposal could have ever been.

Somewhere deep in the walls, I swear I heard Mrs. Grayson give her approval.

Chapter Ninety-Seven

I was adamant. "I really, really, really, and I stress *really* do not want a big wedding. Girls, I'm almost forty. I have grown kids. I can't have frills and froo froo, and I'm not about to waste money on something that I could do for a few bucks at the courthouse."

"But you never had a wedding—at all—like ever," Presley defended her suggestion.

"And Mom, you know we can do a lot of the little stuff at home," Kennedy continued. "We are some pretty crafty ladies." Presley laughed with her.

"I'm not ready to think about that," Travis and I had just told them the news that evening, and after the girly screams and giddy jumping up and down chased him away, I was sitting on the couch with the girls talking about the changes that would surely come.

"Are you thinking summer wedding or even spring? If that's the case we need to do something fast." Excitement filled Kennedy's eyes.

I shook my head. "No way. There is no need to rush this."

"Rush away! You aren't getting any younger."

I threw the pillow at Presley making her laugh even harder. "Well it is true," she whispered loudly to her sister cupping her hand as if to conceal what she said.

I thought for a few minutes and finally told the girls that I thought a winter wedding would be nice, different. That way I had plenty of time to plan, on the small scale that is. I liked knowing there was no time limit, plus I could make sure Mom truly was doing well. We'd be settled in more, getting acquainted with the town and the girls with school. The last thing I wanted was to make Travis a husband and instant dad and scare him away. He needed time to adjust to the girls, with their squeals of excitement and all.

To be truthful I needed time to get used to having a man around full time. Having been single for so long, not even dating in so many years, it would be an adjustment for me as well.

We all needed to adjust. To everything. Just thinking back over the last few months, the last year, I was amazed at the different worlds we were in. We had lived at the beach, now we were in the mountainous area with a lake. We came from a big city to a small town. The schools were different. The people were different. My job was different. We were different. But with all the change came good things. And even if we're twice as different as before, we have twice as much good in our life today than we did back then.

Epilogue

It's been two weeks since the girls left for college. Both decided to stay close to home—our *new* home—and attend Virginia Intermont College. The campus was just over an hour and a half from King Lake. Still too far away if you asked me. I made them promise to come home every weekend—well, most weekends. I needed to make sure they were okay.

Like the move east though, the sports and activities were still not what the girls wanted. Even though Presley didn't have lacrosse, and Kennedy wasn't able to be on a dance squad, both girls found a new love in the Equestrian Club, something they didn't have at Wellington Beach. I could see them asking for a horse or two to join our family in the future.

That would, of course, have to wait. For now, we had just moved from the small apartment above the library to a newly renovated Victorian home in the heart of town. I wanted to remain close enough to Mom to help when needed, and Travis' grandmother had grown up in that home as a child.

It was eight months since Travis and I were married. The girls were successful in talking me into an elaborate winter wedding with their help as my co-wedding coordinators. I was also twenty weeks pregnant, and today we were finding out what our baby's gender would be.

"We *have* to have a boy. I just don't think I can take any more female drama," I said as I tried to get comfortable on the exam chair.

The ultrasound gel, once warmed by the machine, was now cool from the air of the wand as the technician moved it around my abdomen. Travis strained to see the screen, but it was just out of eyeshot for us to get a peak. Maria, the technician explained that measurements and the physical examination came first, then the fun stuff. I was growing impatient.

Finally after ten minutes of anxious silence Marie spoke. "Everything measures and looks great. Did you say something about hoping for a boy?"

"Yes. Is that what you see?" I strained to see around to the front of the monitor.

"Actually, yeah. Congratulations."

Travis and I smiled at each other, and he squeezed my shoulder.

Then Marie continued. "I'm hoping you wanted two, because that's what you have in here. Two healthy boys."

My shocked eyes found Travis' and we agreed on our thoughts in silence.

Oh no. Twins!

KL Palmer calls herself the *working mother's author.*

Even though she hasn't (yet) written a book on how to be a better mom, or how to incorporate your personal life into your long work day; she did follow her dream and write a novel—or three. She hopes to inspire other working moms to write, or follow their dreams wherever they lead, and not give up.

One thing that sets Palmer apart from other authors is her propensity to write with 'break' chapters in mind—chapters short enough to take a bathroom break, commercial break, or smoke break away from life, each averaging two to three pages. She wants to bring reading back into the lives of busy people; to show them you can, in fact, enjoy a book and take time for yourself; and to do so with the limited and precious spare time you have.

Born and raised in a quiet Amish-surrounded community in Pennsylvania, she now resides in Tennessee with her family. In addition to being employed full time in a corporate real estate position, Palmer remains passionate about her church and her writing. She jokes that her mind never shuts off. Even in the most inopportune time she's jotting down ideas for the next manuscript. Just don't tell her boss!

Also Available From

KL Palmer

27 Words
Pipe Dream
The Endurants

Also Available From

WordCrafts Press

Maggie's Song
    by Marcia Ware

The House on Maple Street
    by Marian Rizzo

The Winds of Change
    by Gail Kittleson

Beauty Unveiled
    by Paula K. Parker

Paint Me Fearless
    by Hallie Lee

www.wordcrafts.net